FLAME

DRAGON TRIAD DUET BOOK 2

LANA SKY

Flame

Flame By Lana Sky

ACKNOWLEDGMENTS

Thanks so much to everyone who supported this draft along the way, including the many beta readers who provided encouragement! Please keep in mind that this story includes dark, graphic and explicit content matter that may not be suitable for readers under the age of 18—or for readers who are uncomfortable with the following subject matter: explicit sex, mentions of sexual abuse, mentions of domestic abuse, and graphic depictions of violence.

CHAPTER ONE

I still remember the first time I ever put the tip of my pen to a sheet of fresh paper and scribbled whatever came to mind. What that felt like. In a word? Clarity. I went from voiceless to limitless. My words had power again, however little it might have been.

Amid the deepest depths of my brother's obsession and my parents' indifference, I had an identity all other aspects of my life had stripped away.

I became a *writer*.

For years it's been the one thing I've always excelled at. Creating. Crafting. Emoting.

And yet, lately, it feels like I've run out of the right words. My emotions can't be wrestled onto paper anymore. Gone is that defining identity, and once again, I'm a blob molded by my life circumstances.

So much for being a writer. I can't even voice the truth out loud—the event that, in so many ways, led to this present like the first in a series of falling dominoes.

A story that isn't really mine to tell.

Ironically, I used to imagine what life might be like outside of the cage my past forced me to craft around myself. I just never envisioned this—freedom found in a monster's lair, far different from the one I grew up fearing. *His* world is darker, stranger, lonelier…

And in so many ways, hauntingly beautiful.

I'm a moth, ignited by the intoxicating flame that tempted me to fly so near to it. In the aftermath, all I can do is lie on the ashes of my wings, blinking up at a beige ceiling as my brain struggles to reconcile everything that has transpired within the past forty-eight-hours, ending with me alone in the bed of a man I barely know.

Rafe.

The man embodies so many contradictions it's hard to keep track of them all.

Judging from the coolness of the sheets beside me, I doubt he slept here. I strain my ears, but I don't pick up any noise or footsteps throughout the rest of the apartment, either. The only clue of his presence I find at all, once I creep from his room and down the hall, is an empty cup on the kitchen counter beside a brown paper bag of leftover takeout from last night.

As I approach it, I happen to glance from one of the many windows at the street below. It's too early for rush-hour traffic, but several cars dart past at a steady rate—and my heart lurches at the sight of each one. No matter how hard I try to talk myself out of the growing paranoia, I swear every passing vehicle resembles Branden's.

Is Branden's. Though it's only a matter of time before he comes after me. Running was the stupidest thing I've ever done where my brother is concerned. He requires the same logic my father drilled into me around his hunting dogs— never turn your back. Never let your guard down.

And, most importantly, never give the beasts a reason to chase.

Not that he has to do much work to find me anyway. I spot my phone resting on the coffee table, though I didn't put it there. Ignorant of its use as a tracking device, someone even hooked it up to a charger he must have retrieved from my apartment—though he left it off. That little token of kindness isn't the only one I spy as I rise to my feet and start to pace from room to room.

I spot my shoes beside the door leading downstairs. My toothbrush and toiletries have been left for me on the counter in the bathroom. Three boxes of my belongings sit piled in a distant corner of the hall, rescued from my apartment. Out of consideration, some of my clothing has been neatly folded on the top box for easy access.

That same person probably left my bag within view too. Inside it, I find all those trivial reminders of a life that seems like a stranger's to me now. A crumpled business card and a battered gold lighter are just meaningless trinkets. Even my journal. Its pages are still filled with old writing, including my draft essay for the Fenwick program—my only hope for continuing school in the fall.

The proposed topic? Describe and conquer your inner demons.

I laugh out loud at the idea of it. How pathetic was that? To pin my entire success on a whim. My "talent." Scoffing, I flip the book open and scan the pages. All those pretty, carefully penned words read flat. Empty. Useless, emotionless lies. For the first time in my life, I'm numb as I stroke my thumb along a page. There is no spark.

But one person ensured that I wasn't without this possession anyway—an amount of caring that contrasts sharply with the dark-eyed figure dwelling inside my head. The creature capable of sowing the heavy footsteps I catch advancing up the rickety staircase leading to the apartment's entrance. I know even before the door opens who is behind it. I can smell him—ash and smoke.

His very presence is heralded by a shift in the air, like a drop in temperature warning of a storm. *Rafe.*

"You're awake," he grunts in acknowledgment while closing the door behind him. He's wearing a pair of gray sweats and a white beater top—a casual alternative to his usual jeans and black leather. In his hands is another brown paper bag and a faint aroma emanates from it, making my stomach rumble.

"Come here." With a curt nod, he beckons me into the kitchen where he unloads the contents of his bag on the counter—two steaming breakfast sandwiches wrapped in paper. He hands one to me, claiming the second for himself. As our eyes meet, his expression softens, his lips quirking into a frown.

"You bruise fucking easily, rabbit," he says, stroking my cheek with his thumb. His eyes travel down to my throat, fully exposed by the wide neckline of the shirt I'm wearing now—an oversized black one of his. The earnest sympathy in his tone makes me stiffen self-consciously. Apart from last night, I have no fresher mental image to compare my appearance to.

I can't even look in the mirror.

"Is it that bad?" I ask.

"Damn right," Rafe says, whistling through his teeth. "I doubt even the old 'sunglasses' trick will help you, bunny."

I brush my fingers along my jaw and barely feel any pain. It's like I'm numbed to everything but the here and now. His smell takes precedence over any other sensation, his nearness overwhelming.

Whenever I try to think about the million other pressing concerns in my life, only a few stick out.

"I have to work today," I say absently, though panic sets in at the thought of leaving. Branden will be looking for me, for one. My lease runs out by the end of the week thanks to his efforts. I have no idea how to navigate my usual routine, taking all of that into account. "*That's* what I'm worried about," I add with a tattered laugh. "I have to work today."

"I'll talk to Zhang," Rafe says, referring to my boss. He turns away from me and rummages through the fridge, withdrawing a brown bottle of beer. Despite the early hour, he pops the lid off on the edge of the door and takes a deep swig, throwing his head back.

For the first time, I step outside of my own worries and put myself in his shoes. He looks almost as bad as I feel. I have a sinking suspicion as to why.

"The missing girl. Faith," I say thickly. "You knew her."

"Yeah..." He swipes at his mouth with the back of his hand, his gaze distant. "She was a good kid. What happened to her is fucked up."

He sounds genuinely upset, and I hate the jealousy that unfurls when I try to imagine why. Just how well did he know her?

No better than Branden, a part of me snarls in response. *He's the one who had her hair clip, you idiot.*

Ashamed, I focus my attention to the window as another car drives past. A sharp pain in my hand makes me realize that my fingers are clenched, the nails cutting into my palms. "Do... Do they know what happened to her?" I whisper.

Maybe I'm a masochist, feeding off the weight of the heavy sigh he releases. His obvious regret drills in this reality like a hammer on a nail—this is real.

"Not yet. They found her body on the outskirts of the city, and—" he breaks off with a grimace. "I'll spare you the details."

Traffic is still moving down below, and another car zips by too quickly to inspect in full. I tear my gaze away and find myself staring down the hall instead, toward a stack of boxes. *Tell him,* my conscience warns. *Tell him now.*

"She was in trouble," I say, skirting around the truth again. *Trouble* that wound up with her dead and a piece of jewelry hidden among my belongings. My palms grow slick with sweat at the memory, my pulse increasing. "H-How?"

Rafe grunts, and I turn to find him taking another sip of beer. "She got caught up with the wrong motherfuckers and paid the price for it. And I couldn't help her…"

"Her friend," I say. "The one we saw the night of the vigil. She claimed a man, DW, was the one bothering her—" Not Branden for whatever it's worth. "Do you know who that is?"

"No," he growls. "If I did, I'd be ripping the sick fucker apart, wouldn't I?"

"And Faith never told you anything?"

"I know he's a cop," he says in an icy tone. "And that he was using her somehow. As a drug mule? An informant? I don't know. It's not like I can go ask Gino about it, now can I?" He slams the bottle onto the counter and takes a bite from his sandwich, an obvious clue that he's done talking about it.

For now.

But I can fill in some of the blanks on my own. Faith fell in with his rival Gino—a thug who owns what Mara deemed a "tittie bar." There she met a monster who supposedly made her do awful things.

A monster who found her silence well worth killing her for.

But that doesn't explain why her hair clip is in a shoebox in this very apartment. A threat? A warning? Branden isn't reckless. He took my only other piece of leverage against him, ensuring no one would believe me even if I came forward.

He wouldn't implicate himself in another murder so easily.

So why taunt me with that item in particular?

The more I think about it, the more confusing it all becomes until I'm rubbing at my throbbing temples, trying to make sense of the tangled web.

"Drink," Rafe commands, drawing my attention.

I blink to find the rim of the beer bottle beneath my nose.

"I don't drink," I insist, shaking my head.

"The fuck you don't." Rafe fixes me with another searching look, but one devoid of sympathy. An eyebrow raised, he tilts the bottle toward me again. "Trust me, bunny. You need a fucking drink. You look like shit."

It's the way he says it that makes me inch forward and warily press my lips to the bottle. *Shit,* some level of despair beyond any flowery prose or descriptor.

Satisfied, he manipulates the drink with one hand, allowing me to take the smallest, most cautious sip. It's gross, and I choke down the liquid as he pulls the bottle away.

"Did you sleep?" he asks next.

I shake my head, and he scoffs as though I've insulted him.

"Come on." Grabbing his sandwich, he pivots on his heel, approaching the door.

"Wait…" I contemplate coming clean now. Telling him everything. I *have* to. "I need to tell you—"

"Whatever you want to say, hold it," Rafe snaps with surprising intensity. "I don't want to hear shit until I've eaten." He heads for the stairs, leaving me no choice but to follow.

The second I cross over the threshold after him, paranoia plays a chilling game on my psyche. Branden could be lurking below right now.

Waiting for me.

"It's okay."

I look up to find Rafe halfway down the staircase. "No one's going to fuck with you here," he says.

"You don't know that." My fear isn't faked for the sake of drama. Branden always has a way of controlling me—no matter where I go. Nausea crawls up my throat as I recall the latest example. "He... He's been tracking me through my phone—"

"No one will ever fuck with you here," Rafe insists. "Trust me." He juggles the items in his arms to free up one hand that he extends to me. The fingers are bruised and riddled with scrapes, and yet it's still the most appealing sight I've been presented with all morning.

Finally, I entwine my fingers with his. Rather than head for the front of his shop, he takes me past the back room. There, the short hallway ends at the door leading into a narrow alley. Cool air raises goosebumps over my flesh as we step out into the morning, drawing attention to the fact that all I'm wearing is his shirt, nothing else.

"In here." He opens a nearby door that conceals another staircase. A doorway at the top of it exits onto a wide space beneath the open sky—the building's roof.

With a confidence that betrays just how often he must come here, Rafe guides me forward to a waist-high length of plywood spanning the edge of the rooftop. Below, traffic picks up, and I can't resist scanning every car, hunting for a familiar model.

"Don't," Rafe warns as if reading my mind. "No one can see us up here."

He sits with his back to the railing and arranges his food and drink beside him. "Sit."

Once I do, he grabs his sandwich and takes another ravenous bite. "Eat," he commands with his mouth still full.

I gingerly sample a bite of mine, registering the flavors of sausage, egg, and cheese. "It's good."

But he didn't bring me up here to eat. Blazing in the growing sunlight, his gaze contains a million unanswered questions. Much like a book with a blank cover, it's impossible to discern what he's thinking at a glance. I have to touch him—running my fingers along his forearm the same way I would flip through pages—and tension turns his muscles to stone.

"Damn right, it is," he agrees with my assessment, leaning his head back. His jaw tightens with a hint of seriousness he's concealed until now. "So, tell me… Those cameras I found in your place. Were they your idea or his?"

My cheeks catch fire. The cameras. One in my living room above my TV placed in plain sight. The other, presumably hidden in my bedroom without my knowledge or consent. God only knows what the footage might reveal—me dressing. Undressing. Sleeping…

With Rafe.

"It caught us, didn't it," he suspects in between swigs of his beer. "Is that what set him off?" He nods to indicate my bruised frame. "The fucker watched us."

The thought hurts to explore in full. I have to squeeze my eyes shut and digest it in pieces—Branden, watching me with Rafe. Watching. Watching. Watching.

It doesn't sink in until now as a mangled sound rips from my throat. A laugh? A scream? I'm not sure whether I'm cackling or crying as I bolt onto my knees and vomit.

"Damn." I hear Rafe sigh amid the clink of his bottle being set aside. A heartbeat later, he shocks me—his fingers are in my hair, smoothing stray strands away from my face. "The fucker must have gotten quite the show, huh? Come here."

In his arms, I find a surprisingly warm refuge. Heedless of the mess still dribbling down my chin, he sits back, guiding my head onto his lap.

"Don't let him inside your head," he warns. "That's what he wants. To disgust you. To shame you. He wants you to second-guess the person you are without him. Fuck that."

"You don't sound embarrassed," I croak, finally pegging the sole emotion coloring his voice. Pity for me, but surprisingly no unease for himself. No anger, either. A glance at his face reveals he's sporting his trademark stoic expression. "Or violated."

"I don't have shit to be embarrassed about—" he pauses in his petting of my hair and meets my gaze directly. "You don't either. We didn't do anything wrong."

Conviction resonates in his voice—he truly believes that.

But he doesn't know the awful truth still churning my stomach. Namely, the true identity of "Bran." The way he's watched me for so damn long. The horrible suspicion that planting the camera in my room wasn't done with the sole intention of catching me with someone.

He *wanted* to see me. Control me.

Exploit any part of my life that he could.

"We didn't do anything wrong," Rafe repeats, flexing his fingers as if force alone can drive that fact into my skull. "Sex is sex, bunny. You made your choice to fuck me. I made my choice to fuck you back—and it was damn good."

I flinch at how casual he makes it sound. Like he's said that line before—many times.

"You left last night," I point out, switching to a subject that makes him stiffen this time. He's right. I didn't sleep at all.

But did he?

"Were you with Bonnie?" Would I even have the right to be upset if he had been with the perky blond?

"I was up here," he admits softly.

I observe him more carefully, noting the shadows beneath his eyes I'd missed before. The slight redness to them. He's disguised it so well, but he's wrecked.

"All night?"

He nods. "All fucking night. Any more questions?"

"What were you doing up here?" I glance around the wide space skeptically, but I believe him.

"Thinking," he says, snatching his beer for another sip. His clenched jaw evokes troubles well beyond my personal issues.

"Thinking about Faith?"

He nods.

"And your uncle?"

Irritation flashes across his face. "What about him?"

I struggle to remember some of the conversation I'd overheard between the two. "He wanted you to do something about what happened to her. About Gino—"

"He wants me to do a lot of shit," he says, neither a confirmation nor a denial.

"I heard what he said to you the other night, too," I confess. "He thinks Gino had something to do with Faith's death, doesn't he? And he wants you to confront him. Attack him?"

Or worse.

"Don't worry about him."

"What if... What if Gino didn't hurt Faith?" I suck in a breath, fully prepared to confess the truth. "I—"

"Gino has a motive, but I hope the bastard wasn't that stupid," Rafe says. Going off the low note in his voice, he truly means it. "Whoever killed Faith, I pity the motherfucker. He's a dead man walking."

"Because of your uncle?" I blurt out. I recall how the older man had reacted to the news. As if Faith's death were some kind of personal slight against him.

Rafe shrugs. "Because, bunny, people who do bad shit tend to have it catch up to them eventually. Faith's killer is running out of places to hide."

I bite my lip. Despite everything Branden is, and everything he's done…

Some part of me won't stop clinging to that damn, pathetic phrase—*you owe him.*

"What the fuck were you doing eavesdropping anyway," Rafe demands, thankfully changing the subject.

"I couldn't sleep, and your uncle isn't exactly the quietest person in the world."

"And?" he adds pointedly. "What else did you hear?"

I swallow hard. "And… He doesn't appreciate your art." It seems so childish to point out—but the insult bothers me more than it should. I've seen his drawings. How he looks when in the throes of his craft. I know what the mere act of sketching lines on paper means to him.

Even now, he's tensing, his expression constricted as he chugs more of his beer. At his sides, his fingers twitch as if itching for a pen.

"My turn," he says, once again putting the focus on me. "So, you left him. Bran. What now?"

Any hint of vulnerability vanishes from his expression. His features harden, and a sudden thought strikes me—he already knows what I'll say, or at least he thinks he does.

I need to go back.

"I don't know," I confess, relaxing against the firmness of his knee. "It's not like he left me much of a choice, to be honest. He bought out my lease. The landlord already found a new tenant. I'm homeless. And if I don't figure things out soon, I won't be able to take the classes I want to next semester either."

"Why is that?"

I hesitate, but as his fingers sink through my hair, I find myself speaking. "I wanted to enter this program—the Fenwick program," I admit, fully aware of how childish it sounds now, all things considered. "If I'm accepted, it will mean an internship and a foothold into the publishing world. Otherwise, I'd be stuck taking random credits and waste a year. Though hell, it's not like I had a shot of getting in, anyway."

"Bullshit," Rafe coldly interjects. "You *know* you'll get in. That's what scares you. Getting in means leaving the fucker behind. Whether or not you even realize it, he's controlling you."

My lips part, but any retort I might come up with dies in my throat. He's right, and it's unnerving how easily he can read me. His fingers trace my scalp to reinforce the comparison, picking through my thoughts as though I'm an open book, turning my previous impression of him on its head.

"It doesn't matter if I can't get my entry written in time," I say.

Without some kind of academic pursuit to justify my father's funding, my entire quest for freedom might go up in flames as well. Not to mention if Bran decides to convince him to stop paying my tuition anyway. A tired laugh trickles from me, but inside? I'm screaming.

Branden's won again. Though, despite his efforts, I'm not back in his cage just yet. By pure luck, or by design?

And, despite all his faults, is he really capable of murder?

"You're worried about him," Rafe deduces, unable to hide the jealousy tainting his tone. "Bran."

"He's a cop," I reply. "He's been tracking my phone. He probably already knows I'm here. Any minute he could trump up a warrant and—"

"Cop or not, I won't let anyone touch you."

My body flushes warm in response to his confidence. It's more than a boast.

"You're sure of that?" I peek at him through my lashes, but he doesn't look smug. Just exhausted. "You don't know Bran," I argue.

"Stop. Look at me." He cups my chin, his grip firm but gentle. "I don't care who the fuck he is. No one will touch you while you're with me."

I should counter that. I know the opposite is more than likely—at the same time, I'm too tired to say a word.

In the resulting silence, his hands find my hair again, easing me down against his thigh. Somehow, he makes the position seem far from sexual. Natural, no different from lying in his bed.

Should that insult me?

Thrill me?

"Fine," I finally croak without deciding on an emotion to feel. "So…is this your way of asking me to stay?"

"Stay." He leans back against the railing, stretching out his legs. The motion provides enough surface area to rest on, should I decide to.

"Don't stay," he adds with a shrug. "It's your fucking choice."

I have several reasons to question that—Branden will do whatever he can to get to me, no matter who I'm with. I shouldn't expect so much from a virtual stranger. He's done so much for me already…

Rather than drill him for more answers, I let my eyes drift shut.

Something tells me, given his track record with the truth, I'll find out soon enough.

For better or for worse.

CHAPTER TWO

I will never understand how I manage to fall asleep on literal concrete with my only excuse for a pillow being a toned thigh. In awe, I find myself flexing my fingers over what must be the curve of his knee, resting beneath my chin. It's a marvel how solid he feels. Hard enough to put his fist through glass and pummel a gangster into a bloody pulp. And yet soft enough to comfort me.

In a sense, his body serves as the perfect comparison to his personality—as unpredictable in nature like a chameleon. Or a dragon.

And just like that, my thoughts turn to a far more dangerous topic that haunts me as I trail my hand along his thigh. Like how the contours of this very body felt when pressed against mine. The heat of his skin, slicked by a layer of sweat...

"I'm here for you and all, bunny," a voice cuts into my dreamy haze, constricted with obvious discomfort. "But I am *human*, and while I can tolerate having your head close to my dick for several hours, try to keep those hands to yourself, huh?"

I wrench my eyes open to a blindingly bright stream of sunlight. It's hot out, but my skin feels pleasantly warm. Despite being curled on my side, with my head—as stated—practically on Rafe's lap, I feel utterly content. Which is the complete opposite of how I *should* be feeling.

His mere presence infects me, robbing the seriousness of the moment long enough to almost forget it all. He's staring down on me wryly, his lips quirked upward, betraying a million observations that I suspect he's been stewing over while I slept.

And I did sleep, deeply. A fact that unnerves me when I inspect it too much.

"How long was I out?" I demand, batting my hair from my face as I rise onto my knees.

He shrugs, turning his attention to the brilliant blue sky above. Judging from the position of the sun, it's late morning or even early afternoon.

"About four hours," he says.

"I'm definitely late for work now." With a sigh, I copy his posture by positioning my back against the railing. "Mr. Zhang has a welcome back sale planned. He needs me to help out with the setup."

But I'm not moving.

"I told you—" Rafe fingers the rim of his now empty beer bottle. "I'll handle Zhang. You calling out sick for a few days won't kill him."

"I really do need the money," I add halfheartedly, another wrinkle in the growing web that my life has become. It's laughable how naïve I'd been to think I could extricate myself from Branden's control so easily. "I'll have to start looking for another apartment soon."

An alternate option is asking my father for more money, but I can't even consider it longer than a few seconds.

"You can work for me."

I look over to find Rafe still eyeing the sky, his lips pursed thoughtfully. "At least until you can wear sunglasses."

"Why are you helping me?" I'm genuinely curious—and skeptical.

Any minute, he should toss out some kind of sexual request. Anything to lessen the enormity of what he's really proposing—helping me yet again, for seemingly nothing in return.

"Because I fucking feel like it. Come on—" He stands and inclines his head for me to follow. Once we're back in his shop, he enters the backroom to dispose of our trash. When he returns to my position, his expression triggers a pang of alarm in my chest. I can't decipher it.

"I mean it." His thumb slips beneath my chin when he comes close enough, raising heat in a shiver-inducing swipe.

"You can work for me. At least until you can show your face at Zhang's. I won't even take a cut of your pay."

I raise an eyebrow and wind up wincing with the effort. "Why? And 'work for you' doing what?"

"Well…" He steps into me, and I crane my neck back just to hold his gaze. It's strange how intimidating he can seem when he wants to. Like flipping a switch—all the warmth vanishes from those dark irises, leaving them as unfathomable as the night sky.

"What can you do for me?" He reaches out—but I'm not his target. Instead, he snatches an object from the wall behind me and promptly shoves it against my chest.

A broom.

"You work," he says. "Unlike Zhang, I expect you to earn your fucking keep. I like the place spotless."

"Fine." I curl my fingers around the broom handle as an odd feeling weighs on my stomach, building with every passing second. God, I hate that he can do this to me. Meld fear and gratitude into a disarming mixture that heats my skin and upends my tried and true instincts. His nearness inspires a million nuanced reactions I've never acknowledged before. My frantically beating heart, the rapid breaths causing my chest to rise against the fabric of my shirt. *His* shirt. The rough cotton teases my nipples, hardening them.

And the worst part is that I'm sure he noticed every little detail before I ever did.

"Thank you," I blurt in a rush, still eying the floor.

"Don't." He lumbers into the hall, and I follow him, watching as the pale light emanating from the storefront plays over his skin, reflecting off the subtle hints of gold in it. "Just keep the place spick and span, and I'll… Shit—" he stops short, his shoulders tensing. "Get back."

In a fluid motion, he surges forward, blocking me from view. Through the glass in the door, I can make out the shape of an approaching figure on the other side. Someone tall, wearing a signature shade of navy blue...

My worst fear escapes my lips, uttered in a whisper, "Branden—"

"Hannah," Rafe snaps. "Get back."

His voice knocks some sense into me, and I manage to lurch deeper into the hall, just as he wrenches the door open.

"Officer?" Rafe greets tersely.

I strain my ears to catch the officer's reply, biting my lower lip to choke down any sound I might make. It's Branden.

"Morning," a man replies—but his voice is deep. Too deep to be my brother's. Relief hits me like a bucket of ice water, both bracing and chilling—it's not him. But then who? The silhouette of the figure flung over the far wall is too slender. Not Liam either, but another member of the force. "Are you Rafael Wei-Shen?"

"Figures," Rafe says with a chuckle. "They'd send some newbie who doesn't even fucking know me by name." He laughs again, but the gruff sound triggers an instinctive tug in my stomach. The one that reacts to danger.

Whoever the officer is, he doesn't seem shaken. His shadow doesn't waver, his voice resonating crystal clear. "Are you familiar with a club named Stella's?"

"And if I am?" Rafe replies, but the deliberate second he hesitated before answering alludes that he wasn't expecting this topic to be the cause of the visit.

"Well, are you aware that sometime after one a.m. this morning, a fire was reported at the club?"

"No. But that sounds like a damn shame, officer."

"It is," the officer replies, nonplussed. "Especially considering the club wasn't empty at the time. A man is currently in critical condition, a second barely escaped with minor injuries. And a family of four in a nearby tenant building reported to the hospital for smoke inhalation. Their newborn required oxygen therapy. So you can imagine our alarm that, according to preliminary analysis, it looks like the cause of the fire may have been arson, Mr. Wei-Shen—"

"Wow. That sounds like a *real* damn shame, officer," Rafe snipes. "And not to be rude, but I've got some shit to attend to, and it sounds like you've got some sick motherfuckers to track down. If I have an epiphany, I'll let you know."

"Do that," the man says. "You can also 'let me know' if you recall anything about a young woman named Faith Wen. Her body was found last night. I'm guessing she doesn't ring a bell?"

Rafe says nothing this time, but I can feel his tension even from here.

"I thought so," the officer admits. "Several other women have gone missing under similar circumstances. Were you aware of that?"

"No," Rafe growls.

"When was the last time you recall seeing Faith?"

"Can't remember," Rafe snaps. "Is that all?"

"Strange. Seeing as how you and Faith were so close, at least according to what we've heard. What happened to that poor girl was a real damn shame. We've yet to locate her cell phone either, but you wouldn't know anything about that, would you?"

Rafe scoffs. "That's a really interesting investigation tactic there, officer. Letting a suspect know that you're missing a key piece of evidence."

"Ah, but I didn't say you were a suspect, did I? Have a good day, Mr. Wei-Shen."

As the officer leaves, Rafe slams the door, forming a fist. Without warning, he draws back and slams it knuckles-first against the wall. Again. "Damn it!"

Panting, he pulls away, storming in my direction.

"Did you do it?" I'm standing in his way, but I can't seem to move. A sense of dread pools in my chest. Or maybe it's relief? I should be begging for a reason to hate him. Doubt him.

Will he lie to me? *Did* he lie to me?

"Did you set the fire?"

"I don't know…" He takes another step, towering over me, his gaze unreadable. "Did I, rabbit? Would I be sloppy enough to set a fucking fire that would bring the cops right to my doorstep? Or would I be a little bit smarter than that?"

His gruff tone differentiates this anger from his usual temper. Rather than rage and shout, he has his jaw clenched, his eyes distant. He's just as on edge as I am.

Why? His wary glance toward the front of the shop might give me a clue. "Those motherfuckers," he hisses. "What the fuck are they up to…"

It hits me—if his uncle's men were behind the attack, he didn't know. And the prospect caught him off guard. Did the older man leave him out intentionally?

Or was Rafe the one who stayed away?

The questions mount, but all I seem capable of doing is sighing, still clenching his broom.

Eyeing him, I press the bristles to the floor. "When do I start?"

"Huh?" He blinks and shoots me an odd look, only to recover a heartbeat later. His slanted smirk contains a mere fraction of his usual smug persona, however. He's distracted. "You start now," he says. "But change first. I'm not running a fucking skin bar."

He boldly rakes his gaze down to my bare legs before starting for the stairs. I follow him into the apartment and approach the clothing stacked on top of the boxes at the end of the hall. I grab a skirt and sweater only to draw a scoff from my audience.

"I don't run a nunnery, either," Rafe says, reaching around me to snatch the sweater away. His breath heats the back of my throat, his voice vibrating through my skin, "Trust me. You look better in my shit."

Referring to his shirt, I presume. The possession in his words requires further inspection—but later. For the time being, I squeeze past him and enter the bathroom, closing the door behind me.

He retreats, his steps storming toward the living room with a determination that alarms me. At least until I hear his voice, low, strained, presumably speaking into a phone.

"...If I hear you motherfuckers were involved, I swear to God," he growls. "You'll answer to me. I told you to keep out of this—I don't give a fuck what anyone might think.

Just be ready when those assholes come calling, because they will."

Judging from the next few seconds of silence, he must have hung up.

"Hurry up, bunny," he calls, raising his voice for my benefit. "I don't got all fucking day."

"I'm coming," I snap back.

Approaching the mirror is a grueling ordeal, but in the end, I don't even look at my reflection. I grab a washcloth from a nearby shelf and wash up blind. Once finished, I tug on my skirt and fresh underwear. I finally exit the bathroom to find Rafe standing near one of the windows in the living room with his back to me.

"What's the rush?" I ask, crossing my arms. "Are you—"

"Fuck." His posture alone conveys another alarming shift in his mood. Gone is the mocking, playful aura. "Shit's about to get real, bunny," he says coldly, his gaze riveted on something taking place below.

"What's wrong?" I ask.

As I inch closer to the window, I spot the problem for myself—a parade of three, flashy cars parking alongside the curb across the street. As if in some rehearsed motion, the driver's side doors open in sync, and the occupants stream out. They're dressed in suits—and I instantly recognize their leader.

Gino.

The other men with him are unfamiliar, but they approach the shop with a clear intent made obvious by their posture —clenched fists and rigid spines. Nothing good.

"Fuck." Rafe barrels into the kitchen, speaking to me from over his shoulder. "Can you shoot?"

"What?" I gape as he wrenches open a cupboard drawer and rummages through the various random items inside it. *Shoot* could apply to a milieu of different things—or so I try to convince myself.

At least until he slams an object onto the counter, leaving nothing to the imagination. A part of me knows what is inside the slim black case before he lifts the lid.

"Rafe…" I back away, but my alarm doesn't prevent him from curling his fingers around the hilt of the weapon and raising it—a gun.

I've seen one before—my brother's service weapon. This one looks to be a similar model, black and no less intimidating.

"What's going on—"

"You hear shit going down, you take this, and you run," he says as if I've never spoken. "Get the fuck away—but if you can't, get on the roof. Do you hear me? Listen!" He smacks the counter with his free hand. "Do you remember that place you brought Zhang's payment? Do you?"

I nod, picturing a musty warehouse on the outskirts of town, by the docks.

"Good. You get there, and you wait for me. If I don't show, you look for a red case. I already changed the combination to something you'll be able to guess, and you—"

"You're scaring me," I croak.

"You're damn right, I am." He returns the gun to the case, closes it, and sets it on the counter. "Remember this shit—"

A sound erupts from down below. One, ironically, we're both familiar with—smashing glass.

"Damn it." He pushes past me and wrenches open the door to the stairs. "Keep an ear pressed to the goddamn floor if you have to. You hear me say 'motherfucker' in any context, you run. You don't hesitate. There's a fire escape below the window in the hallway. Got it?"

"Rafe—"

"You fucking listen." He holds my gaze until I finally nod.

"Okay," I rasp.

Satisfied, he pivots and descends the steps, slamming the door behind him.

My pulse hammers against my eardrums, filling the silence left in his absence—but the quiet doesn't last long. A series of footsteps resonate through the building's very foundation, heading toward the shop's front.

"What the fuck do you want?" I hear Rafe demand.

"You son of a bitch!" I recognize the speaker as Gino, his voice constricted with rage. "Do you have any idea of what you've done? Who you've fucked with? Do you?" More glass shatters in a musical cacophony. The frames holding his drawings? Something bigger? Panic chokes me, and this sense of blindness only enhances my dread. I'm shaking, my knees knocking together, my gaze fixated on the floor as if I can see through it by sheer willpower. What did he tell me?

You hear me say 'motherfucker' in any context, you run.

I drop to my knees, bracing my hands against the floorboards. Too suddenly—I might be heard from down below. I hold my breath, fearing just that, and I strain my ears, listening for any hint of what's happening.

"…think you can fuck around with us?" another man demands. "You stupid cunt. You have no idea what you've started."

"I don't, do I?" Rafe sounds more distant as if he's speaking from the very front of the store now. "Tell the bitch holding your leash that he doesn't know what *he's* done. Faith Wen? That name ring a bell? The next time you whore out your girls for a dime, don't get so goddamn sloppy. I went easy on your ass once. No more."

"You think you know everything, huh?" Gino replies with a harsh bark of laughter. "Oh, this is well beyond Faith, you dumb son of a bitch. You have no idea who you've *really* fucked with, do you?"

"Do you?" Rafe snarls amid the sound of more smashing glass. Each tingling chime brings to mind a series of picture frames breaking one by one. "I know the assholes you cater to. Bastards who strongarm barely legal girls into sex. Who torture them. Then kill them to protect their fucking reputations—"

"Faith was a lying little cunt," Gino snarls. "She stuck her nose into where it didn't belong. But it's not like you have any *proof.*" He deliberately emphasizes the word with a hiss. "Do you, Rafael? Hidden in this rundown piece of shit? Keep looking," he snaps, presumably to his men.

"Go fuck yourself," Rafe snarls. "If she did give me anything, do you think I'd be dumb enough to keep it here?"

"You better hope not. Though maybe you need a little convincing to tell the truth? Boys. Hold him."

Thuds erupt, alluding to a struggle, but sheer terror roots me in place. I can't move. Can't breathe…

My gaze drifts to the counter, and the box resting there, as my ears strain for a key phrase. Would I have the strength to grab it even then? I try to make my hands move, but my fingers twitch in place and nothing more.

"Fuck," Rafe snarls, and the pain in his tone sets every nerve on red alert. He's hurt.

I'm already on my feet, scrambling for the counter. I wrench open the box and clumsily grasp the object inside it. As I turn to the door, a shout rings out.

"Fuck! You motherfuck—"

"Shit!" Another man says. "Someone must have called the fucking cops."

Cops. That word spurs my paralyzed limbs into motion, and I creep toward the window. Sure enough, a lone cruiser idles alongside the curb. I'm not sure if it's the same one that used to live in Branden's driveway, polished to shine.

From this height, I can't make out the driver or anyone in the passenger seat. Liam?

The sound of a door slamming reinforces the more pressing danger. Three figures trickle from the store and stroll across the street. One man, in particular, has his hands in fists, visible from even here. A substance glistens over the prominent knuckles, and my mind goes blank with recognition. Blood.

By the time I regain my senses, I'm already inching down the short hallway on the first floor, tensing in expectation of what I might find beyond it. The smell reaches my nostrils first—coppery, fresh…

"R-Rafe?" From my vantage point, I can only make out the shattered front door at first—the source of much of the glass scattered across the floor. Anxiety builds with every step I take.

Near the counter, I spot a sight that almost makes me drop the item in my grasp. Rafe—upright, clutching at his chin. Overwhelming relief blinds me to anything else. Like self-preservation. I pick through a sea of broken glass to reach him on bare feet, heedless of the risk.

"Are you okay?" The words have barely left my mouth when I realize that he isn't. Blood is gushing from his lower lip. A lot. He may need stitches, though I'm already setting the gun aside and winding up the hem of his shirt to use as a makeshift cloth.

"I'm fine," he grunts, shrugging off my attempts to dab away the blood—until suddenly he isn't. We're face to face, toe to toe, and I suck in a breath, my hands frozen with his shirt lifted high enough to expose my stomach. For once, he drops the bravado. His face reveals everything—every emotion he's hidden so well until now.

Fear.

"They were here about the fire," I deduce, dabbing at his jaw as I remember how to move again. "And Faith."

He dodges my touch, his eyes narrowing. "I guess I told you to eavesdrop this time, so the joke's on me."

"Yes," I say thickly. "So, stay still."

He grudgingly submits to the ministrations but snatches the gun and slips it into his pocket. Thankfully, a split lip seems to be the extent of his injuries. Not that knowing as much stops my fingers from running over his forearm without my brain telling them to, searching for any hint of damage there.

When I reach his shoulder, he gently bats my hand away, swiping at the remnants of blood with his bare hand. "It's broad fucking daylight, and those assholes came *here*," he hisses, sounding more incredulous than infuriated. "Even you were smart enough to grab a weapon, though I don't know how you'd shoot it with the safety on. Shit. You know it as well as I do—this is about more than a fucking fire, bunny."

"Tell me, then," I demand. The back of my neck prickles with an awareness of just how dangerous a request this is.

Some monsters and their secrets are best left in the dark.

Regardless, watching his dark eyes scan the carnage of glass scattered at his feet triggers the same instinctive pull that I felt the night when I stole his lighter. In a childish sense, I'd believed I'd been protecting it from him. What had my rationale been? Some monsters *deserve* protecting…

"I want to know," I insist. The hitch in my voice contradicts that confidence. To steel myself, I tiptoe back into the hall in search of the one task I can do as I await his response. I find the broom where I'd left it. Grasping it in both hands, I return to the front and get to work sorting out the pieces of glass too small to pick up.

It's monotonous work—nearly distracting enough to shield me from his presence. He's watching me, his gaze like a laser, piercing through flesh and bone.

"What do you want to know?" he asks, though I get the sense that he's mocking me.

I look back to find his gaze far more serious than I expect, though.

Sighing, I lift my shoulders. "Everything."

He leans against the counter, letting his lip bleed freely. Confidence enhances him, until he's a giant, invincible amongst a sea of destruction.

"My uncle calls his outfit 'red dragon' though he's not stupid enough to broadcast it. Most of the people around here know he's dirty. They just don't know how." His gruff inflection conceals a dare.

One I warily take him up on. "So how?"

"Extortion, money laundering. Worse," he says with a coarse laugh. Shaking his head, he runs his fingers through his hair. "I can't believe I'm fucking spilling the dark family secrets to a nosy little bunny. You still could be a fucking reporter."

But he's talking to me. Deep down. I suspect that he needs to do just that. Talk. To someone. Anyone.

"He has a protection racket going, but it's just pocket change," he says. "His real money comes from real estate these days. Cleaning up his image so he can make a jump into politics. To hear him tell it, he's too 'reformed' to get his hands dirty anymore."

"Do you?" It chills me to the bone that I don't truly know what I'm asking. Dirty hands could refer to so many things.

Judging from the distant, cold gleam in his eyes, I suspect that none of the answers he could give I'd find reassuring.

"I work for him," he says softly. "Take that however you fucking want. Does that make me his errand boy? Probably.

But he promised me he's getting out of the business soon. Besides, he's family."

But there's more to it, apparent in what he doesn't say.

"So what happened with Gino?"

"Gino and his pathetic excuse for a wanna-be-mafia have been muscling in on our territory for years," he says. "His old man worked with Shen back in the day. They were partners, but lately, the bastard's gotten too cocky. He has a deal extending from his shitty club all the way to the top. Cops. Politicians. They come to his club for pussy and pay through the nose for it—but that's just the start of it. You see these cops, in return for the shit they get away with, overlook whatever happens in Gino's part of town. Murders. Disappearances. Everything. The fish rots from its fucking head—they're all in on it."

Anger leeches into his voice that was absent when he spoke of his uncle. Whatever his issue with Gino is, it's personal.

And he seems to feel that same animosity toward the police.

"You doubt that?" he prods, sensing my discomfort. "Your precious Bran is one of them. You ever hear him talk about hanging around Stella's?"

His tone is cutting—he wants a fight. Rather than give him one, I turn my attention to a pile of toppled frames in the corner and stoop to salvage what I can. Which isn't much. Only one casing is wholly unbroken, containing the snarling image of a wolf with mistrustful eyes.

It reminds me of Branden. For all I know, he could be in the cruiser still parked outside. I'm torn between alerting Rafe to its presence or just letting the inevitable take place.

The more I run, the harder he'll give chase.

"This is beautiful," I murmur, spotting another drawing, clinging to the distraction it provides.

"That bother you?" Rafe calls, like a shark catching a whiff of a drop of blood. "That your perfect boyfriend—that *Bran* could be a part of that shit? Trust me, chances are more likely than not that he is, bunny—" a fact he seems to gloat over. "Maybe you don't know him like you think you do."

"I know Bran better than anyone." And *that's* why I'm shaking. Why the back of my throat feels tight with the threat of vomit. I know Bran.

Could he be involved in something so heinous? Ironically, Rafe hit on the answer himself—the chances are more likely than not.

"Come here," he commands.

As I advance toward him, he withdraws the gun, presenting it to me on the flat of his palm. I jump, but the look in his eye banishes any alarm I might feel.

"You think the bastard cares about you," he says, once again reading me like an open book. "But he didn't even teach you to fucking shoot? A cop should be good for that much." He jerks his chin, daring me to inch closer.

The second I'm close enough, he snatches my waist with his free hand, spinning me so that my back hits his chest as he lowers the gun before me.

"Grab it."

I do with both hands, hating the weight of it. The power conveyed in the trigger.

Disgust inspires another confession from me, "I never wanted to learn."

Rafe laughs. "Fuck that. You need to. Hold it like this—" he guides my fingers into the right positions. "The gun isn't bad, bunny. Just make sure that you never point it at something you aren't willing to destroy. Kill. It's the intent that matters. Like when you write those pretty little words of yours—but in this case, there is only one conclusion to take away."

"And what's that?" I whisper.

"That you decide what happens next," he says, coaxing me to aim at the wall near one of his still hanging sketches—a snarling dragon. "You are in control of good or bad. It's all on you. So, learn how to take the safety off at least."

He demonstrates how with a few flicks of his thumb. Then he pulls away entirely, and I turn to find him stowing the weapon behind the counter.

"You seem comfortable with that," I deduce as my brain taunts me with why that might be. "Have you shot someone before?"

He grunts, palming the counter. "Don't ask me questions you don't really want to know the answer to."

Fair enough.

"Do you teach all of your women how to operate a weapon?" I ask.

Let alone in, as he put it, "broad daylight," in the middle of his vandalized shop. The fact that the police aren't swarming this place stuns me. A glance through the shattered door reveals no one in sight. The city itself might as well be deserted.

And the idling cruiser never does anything more than that. Wait.

"Teach the others? No. Only the sexy little bunnies who play out the innocent shtick," he counters. But his tone is too hard to be mocking. He's still on edge. Worried.

"What's wrong?"

He meets my gaze from over his shoulder. "What happened just now? That was just a friendly kiss on the cheek, bunny —they'll be back. And if you do decide to stay, you better be ready for that. Gino is a ticking time bomb. It's only a matter of time before the idiot goes too far."

If I stay…

There are plenty of reasons why I shouldn't, but I can't dwell on the choice now—so, I retrieve the broom, and I perform the one task I have control over. I clean.

Ironically, there is some familiarity in the act where he is concerned. I'm transported back a few days ago when I dutifully scrubbed blood stains from the floor of my old apartment. Utilizing the broom, I push the smallest pieces of glass into the center of the room, letting the monotony lull my brain into a false sense of normalcy.

Nothing else matters. Like the fact that I'm essentially homeless, or the police cruiser slowly driving away without its occupant ever stepping foot from it.

Once I've made headway in sorting a majority of the glass, I finally take stock of the store as a whole.

"So much for your invitation-only policy," I state to Rafe, nodding to the remains of the front door. "You may have to take walk-in clients, after all."

He shrugs and lumbers down the back hallway, muttering over his shoulder, "I have plywood somewhere."

A few minutes later, he returns armed with sheets of the material while I set off in search of a dustpan.

Between the two of us, it takes only a few hours to have a majority of the mess either boarded up or filed away into trash bags. Only as I dump the last few shards of glass into a quickly filling bag do I gather up the nerve to broach the topic he himself left open for discussion, "You said I can ask you anything."

He's on the other side of the room, wrestling the larger frames into a trash bag. Stopping, he looks back at me. "And?"

I suck in a breath, mulling over how to phrase my next question. But there isn't a pretty way to put it. "Mara says you're a member of the triad."

"Triad?" Laughing, he approaches me and lifts my chin with the pad of his thumb, peering directly into my eyes. "Do you even know what that word fucking means, bunny?"

I don't break eye contact. "I know it sounds illegal."

"Illegal." His voice deepens, raspier than usual. "Do you even know what *that* word means, rabbit? It means I do shit like 'shake down old men for money,' right? Or it could mean that I pay off their debts when a little bunny bats her eyes at me once. It means…"

Suddenly, he's too close. Warm breath feathers over my skin, and with every inhalation, his nostrils flare as if straining for more of me. More, more, more. I eye the flames licking down his forearm, convinced the dragon suits him more than ever. This must be how such a predator chooses to devour his prey—through fire. One scorching exhale at a time.

He even resembles the creature. Dark, glowing eyes and a fearsome expression unbothered by the day's events. Jealousy bites at my fragile resolve. Even bruised, he looks unshaken. Untouchable.

I look…

Broken. A trembling little bunny shrinking from my own reflection. But in his eyes, there is no hiding from it. The real Hannah is laid bare in the center of his irises—a creature caught beneath his gaze with a wide, unwavering expression. Someone who makes his brow furrow and his lips part, glistening with wetness.

The motion draws my attention to the red gash there—no longer bleeding—and the trail of dried blood snaking down his jaw.

I don't know why I do it. Lick my forefinger and swipe at the smear. Maybe self-preservation? Scarlet suits him, feeding the dangerous illusion he struggles to maintain. Without it, he's no more intimidating than anyone else.

Though no one has these eyes. Dark, they meet mine unflinchingly as he gently captures my hand in his. And no one has his voice, inspiring goosebumps as it drips into my ear. "I'll tell you," he murmurs, picking up the thread of our previous conversation. "It means I'm capable of some fucked-up shit, bunny. Shit that would make your innocent little toes curl. It means…you should probably vet the people you fuck."

"You too," I counter in a tone I don't recognize. "You don't know me."

He blinks in surprise before releasing a low laugh. "I figured that," he snarls, lowering his mouth to the crook of my shoulder. "I knew from the second I first saw you, watching me with those bunny eyes—you're a head fucker. I've got my work cut out, don't I? Making sure you don't pull your tricks on me—"

He seizes a piece of sore, abused skin, and rakes his teeth over it. In the same moment, he captures my waist, anchoring me to him. My nails sink into his forearms, seeking out stability, but beneath the various aches and pains I still feel all over my body, something sparks to life, too foreign to name. Pleasure?

Whatever it is builds as his lips latch over my pulse point, his tongue lathing in slow strokes.

It's terrifying how easily I can forget everything else.

"You get off on this," he grates, exhaling against my collar. "The thrill of it all. But you should ask yourself, bunny… What happens when I decide I'm tired of playing with you?"

In so many ways, it feels like a rhetorical question. One even he doesn't know the answer to—because he's the one initiating this game. His fingers are already sliding beneath the hem of my borrowed shirt, drifting to the waistband of my skirt and grazing the flesh beneath. Then he changes tack and travels higher. His fingers find my breasts next, toying with my nipples until I can't silence a gasp.

Our lips meet, and it's electric. My skin flushes warm as his tongue coaxes my mouth open before slipping inside. At the same time, his fingers continue their slow, searching caress unabated. I find myself arching into him, extending every moment—his touch, his taste.

But right before the inferno can truly take hold, I draw back.

Good, a part of me urges. *You should stop. You have too much to worry about. Branden. The program. Everything. This can only distract you for so long…*

Rafe tenses as if expecting me to voice that very conclusion.

But around him, I can't even predict myself anymore. A question escapes my mouth without any input from my brain, "Is the bed off-limits?"

CHAPTER THREE

H e frowns, his eyes narrowing. Abruptly, he snatches my wrist, pulling me down the hall and up the stairs into his apartment. We cross the living room, heading straight for an infamous door that he doesn't hesitate to push open.

The bedsheets are still rumpled from when I last slept in here, the room otherwise unchanged. I cross the threshold as a dominating figure steps into me from behind. His hands return to my thighs, gripping them tightly before inching up to my shirt. He drags the fabric along with his ascent, baring my body to the cool air.

Removing my skirt is his next task. Warm, his fingers curl around my wrists after, guiding me to the end of the mattress. He leans into me from behind, forcing me onto my stomach beneath his weight. The firm flesh of his chest rasps over my bare back as his lips settle into the crook of my shoulder.

"You want this, bunny?" he asks near my ear.

Eager, I reach back, digging my nails into his skin without remorse, relishing the dangerous sound that revs up in his chest. He doesn't need a violent invitation, anyway. A part of me shivers beneath the ominous knowledge of what's coming, but he surprises me by drawing out the gentleness a moment longer. His fingers dip between my legs and stroke me luxuriously, as if he's just a normal man, and this is a normal roll in the hay.

I almost believe it. I let myself go limp, shuddering on the edge of an orgasm, my lips pursed to smother any sound I might make. The first shudders begin to wrack my body when he flips me over onto my back and settles on top of me. Cool air replaces his hand while he rakes his nails over my torso. Hard.

"Watch." There's a dark note in his tone, and I tremble with recognition. The man who bathed my wounds is gone. A dragon comes to life in his place, its hot breath igniting my skin. Aware of where his gaze is traveling, I struggle to prop myself on both elbows and stare. My breath catches at the sight of his fingers between my legs, the knuckles threatening to push inside me. He's hunched over, his expression unashamed as he takes me in, sweeping his gaze along the naked length of me. "Don't look away."

He strips his shirt, and the lines of his tattoo consume his forearm, leaving snippets of golden skin. It makes him seem as wild and untamed as the creature on his back. Ethereal.

I can sense the restraint he uses to guide my legs further apart, leaving himself enough space to crouch down between them. Then his fingers return, dipping inside me one after the other. So damn carefully, it's like he knows I'll shatter beneath too much pressure.

Watch.

I can't seem to tear my gaze away, but the sight doesn't affect me nearly as much as the sound. The soft groans he grits out between clenched teeth. The way his breath catches when I arch my hips, urging him deeper. The creak of the mattress, protesting under our combined weight.

"Lie on your back."

I comply without complaint, and my eyes are on the ceiling when he slides two fingers inside me. Quick. Hard. The fullness is an entirely new sensation, burning painfully and pleasurably at the same damn time. I fumble for a fist full of the bedsheets and grab hold, just as he begins to thrust. In and out—more forcefully each time.

My thoughts splinter. My body quakes. Fire sweeps through my veins, and it's almost enough to make me forget.

Everything.

"Rafe…" His name is a prayer, but I don't know for what. For less? More? As if to punish me, he draws out the last thrust, forcing me to feel every inch of his presence. The firm ridges of each knuckle. The callouses. The scars. I'm drugged with the sensation of him, feeling his touch translate to the words he doesn't voice out loud—*I own you this way—only me.*

I gasp out loud when he finally withdraws them, and his hand approaches my mouth. "Open."

Disgust and alarm converge into a refusal that springs to the tip of my tongue—but then I see his face. Those eyes, burning with a fire that leaves me senseless.

My mouth opens, and he swipes the slick pad of a thumb along my lower lip. My tongue drifts up before I can help it, catching the edge of his nail. He lets me lap at his fingertips at first, while darkness consumes what remains of his irises. When the last drop of humanity finally fades, he shoves them all in so hard I nearly choke.

Gagging, I struggle to suck, tasting myself on him, along with sweat. Maybe a hint of blood. I don't feel as disgusted as I should. Perhaps I'm not at all. I can't make up my mind before he pulls his hand away, leaving a moist trail that splatters my chest, and rears back on his knees. Taking the back of my calves in either hand, he spreads my legs.

The muscles in his arms ripple as he wrenches down his sweatpants, and I take him in with greedy glances, grateful for the fading sunlight seeping in. The golden glow gives me just enough light to appreciate the definition in the muscles of his upper thighs as he finally settles over me and pushes in.

I bite my lip. He's still going slowly, and I'm grateful for the reprieve, almost as much as I'm anticipating what's coming.

It's the first time I've gotten the chance to savor him like this. To actually process the feeling of him inside me. The hungry way my body clamps over him. The way his jaw clenches in response, his eyes glowing. The sounds he makes in that beautiful voice as he eases the head of himself all the way in and then begins to thrust in earnest.

He continues to take his time, easing his length inside me, stretching me fully. There's one last shred of gentleness as he hooks his hand around the back of my head and brings his face in close. With heart-stopping tenderness, his lips seek mine out, but the kiss doesn't last long. My lips burn when he pulls away and flips me over, forcing me to prop myself up on trembling hands.

He uses his fingers to spread me apart and then enters me again. Hard. The friction burns, and I grit my teeth, my eyes watering as he pulls back and then thrusts again. It's rough. He loses the steady rhythm, causing the mattress to shudder beneath us. I have to reach for a handful of the sheet and bite down just to keep from crying out. One of my hands fumbles for the headrest and finds a groove between the wall and the headboard. I curl my fingers around the metal and hold tight as he rocks his hips, jarring me forward.

I count the harsh slaps of flesh against flesh. *One. Ten. Twenty.* Despite the violence, my body heats up. Already, I can sense another orgasm is just out of reach, licking impatiently at my skin. My toes curl. I gulp for air. He's still thrusting when his fingers return to my clit, rubbing, pinching, stroking…until the intensity of my release slams into me. It knocks me over. My cheek hits the mattress. My ass is in the air, my body still at his mercy.

For what feels like an eternity, I just let him use me. Each thrust carries his rage, filling me up. Overflowing from every pore. Drowning me with the emotion. I'm just a vessel for his anger, willing, and receptive.

Already my body starts to ascend again, and I hate myself for the fact that the harsher the thrust, the higher I climb. I swear my head hits the ceiling as his thumb maneuvers between my legs, flicking, stroking. Faster. Higher. I fly apart beneath his fingertips before he ever starts to fuck me in earnest.

Wordless moans spill into the cotton clamped between my teeth, and when he speaks again, he sounds miles away.

"Move." The command is bitten out against the back of my neck. The hand between my legs drifts up to grasp my shoulder, forcing my spine to arch so that he can hover over me, his chest against my back, altering the angle. I gasp when he swivels his hips, and the bitten sheet falls from my mouth.

The penetration isn't nearly as deep as before, but the sensation is harsher. Damn near explosive. Sparks shoot through my body with every exacting stroke of his, alighting every nerve.

Setting me on fire.

I've never been so raw in my life. So wet. I can't seem to find any air, but it doesn't really seem to matter. He slams life into me—marks me with jabs from an invisible knife that will never ever heal. And I relish every single wound. When he's inside me, I'm not some pathetic, helpless rabbit.

I'm not even sure I'm still human. I'm greedy. I'm restless. Reckless. My nails seize hold of a pillow, digging in as I flex my hips toward him, meeting every thrust and eliciting hungry growls that resonate in my skin.

"That's it." He voices his pleasure in a low groan when my inner muscles clutch him, urging him to spend himself. Empty every bit of emotion from his body that he can't control. *Use me.*

"Bunny." His fingers latch onto the back of my skull, tugging my head toward him. The moment I'm within reach, his teeth seize my ear, nipping while his other hand cups my breast, squeezing just on this side of pain. He curses when I moan, the foreign words he mutters somehow making sense in my lust-addled brain.

"You're mine."

My sweat-soaked fingers lose their hold over that groove in the headboard. I settle for bracing both hands flat on the sliver of mattress in front of me, riding him until it doesn't matter if we're silent or not. The headboard rams against the wall, and I can't muster the energy to care.

Doubt fades. Shame melts away, and I surrender to everything he has to give. The fingers of his other hand find my nipple, swiping it into a stabbing peak before doing the same to the other.

And then I feel him slam into me with a shudder and the world ceases to matter.

Noises crawl from my throat I've never heard myself make, melding with his deeper, gruffer grunts. It's a symphony of pure, primal pleasure. My fingers grip his forearms, tracing the path of the flames spewing from the creature on his back as his explanation for designing it echoes in my mind —*it's power. Control.*

Another word seems fitting enough to describe it as well— *it's freedom.*

But it doesn't last. His thrusts quicken, losing their punishing rhythm. He grits his teeth on a frantic pace toward release—but his hand slips between us, finding a part of me that makes my spine curl as if connected to an invisible tether. One he can command with stroke, after stroke, after stroke…

Until he finally stills, his mouth at my throat, his fingers twisting through my hair.

"Fuck," he hisses before rolling off me to collapse onto his back. "Holy fuck."

He doesn't sound happy, just exhausted. I look over to find him scowling up at the ceiling, his chest heaving in a ruthless tandem to match his panting breaths.

It's jarring how he switches out emotions. Fire one minute and ice the next.

"You had to fuck him." He chuckles to himself, wiping his hand over his injured lip. "It would certainly explain why he's so damn pussy-whipped. You had to fuck him…"

I don't follow the leap in logic, but the confidence in his voice unnerves me enough to let another piece of the truth slip free. "It was never like that with him…"

He frowns and shoots me a searching glance. "It was about control, then. Getting inside your head. Directing your every move. That's what he got off on."

"It wasn't like that, either," I whisper.

Though he's not far off. I've spent my whole life growing accustomed to Branden's control. One mantra above all was drilled into my head like a creed. I owed him.

"Our… My parents never really looked out for me," I admit, stretching out onto my back beside him. "They were successful. We were wealthy. But my mom had her issues, and she wasn't around much when I was growing up. My dad was overwhelmed and looked to other relationships to cope. Branden was the one left to look out for me." It sounds strange when said out loud. Dysfunctional. In reality, it was all we knew. "One day… I think I must have been five. I ran out into the street and was almost hit by a car. The fallout was bad. The police were called. They couldn't find my parents. Bran was twelve, and it hit him hard. Things looked worse than they were. The aftermath could have ruined his life."

"He doesn't sound like your boyfriend," Rafe says. Strangely, he doesn't accuse me of lying outright. His tone carefully straddles the line between confusion and irritation, leaving it entirely up to me whether or not to come clean.

But there's no point in denying it anymore.

"He's not. Bran is my brother," I confess, too weary to even see how that piece of information lands. I stare up at the ceiling, my thoughts like a sieve, leaking all of the dark memories I've struggled to suppress.

"So what? Your parents got busted for neglect. Why the fuck is that your problem?"

I hesitate to answer, squeezing my eyes shut against the past. "Because… I wasn't wearing any clothes." The silence that falls in the wake of those words is deafening. The only way to combat the awkwardness is to keep talking. "And I don't remember what I said when the police came, but they were concerned enough to start an investigation. I shouldn't have to say what kind."

"Shit," Rafe says.

I nod in agreement. "All of that because of me." It always surprises me how deep the guilt goes. How a child's innocent actions could lead to a whirlwind of chaos.

"Bran had to go see a child psychologist after that because of me. I was almost put into foster care. My parents were mortified. I could have ruined his life—"

"Did he touch you?" Rafe demands.

I flinch at how earnestly he asks that question. "No! Not like that. Not—"

"You were a kid." His anger startles me. I open my eyes to find him tense, his eyes darker than ever. "A kid who ran out of your house *naked*."

"It wasn't like that," I insist, shaking my head. "I was probably playing a game or something. I barely even remember—"

"And how many years later and the bastard beats you. He hides a camera in your fucking room. Shit, he *watched* you naked!"

I cringe. "Stop making it sound like…"

"Like what? Like he may have molested you? That he's still abusing you. Trust me, it's not that hard to spell it out."

I roll onto my side as if shielding my body from view can protect from his judgment. "Stop!"

But he's too riled. Hissing, he brandishes a fist at nothing, his eyes flashing. "And your parents? They let you go around believing that shit? That you owe him because of what he did?"

"It's not that simple," I insist.

"Bullshit!" He strikes the mattress so hard I jump. "The fuck it's not. And what about that story you wrote, huh? Deceiver? What the fuck is that about? Did he hurt someone in front of you?"

"Please stop," I plead as my voice breaks. "I've never told anyone this."

Because I know how it sounds—and I know what dark turn this story eventually takes.

"You don't know what it's like," I add. "To be chained to someone, and you can't explain why. But it's what it is."

"Is it?" he snarls. "Why the fuck did you have a heart after his name in your phone then. Huh?"

I feel my cheeks flame as I choke out the answer, "Because it was one way to remind myself that despite everything he's done... I shouldn't hate him. I can't hate him."

"Fuck..." Rafe sighs, and some of the tension drains from his muscles. Judging from his tight expression, those words resonated with him more than I expected. Finally, he cocks his head at me, his gaze focused. "You said he tracked your phone?"

I nod, alarmed as he stands and crosses to his dresser, still naked. The dragon on his back ripples, coming to life as he wrenches open a drawer.

"Well, let's give the fucker something to follow." He tosses me a wad of fabric—another shirt. "Put it on," he demands while stepping into a pair of jeans. By the time I remember how to move, he's already storming into the living room. He grabs my phone from the coffee table and marches for the door, snatching something from a small hook hanging beside it on his way out.

"Wait!" I scramble into my sandals, grab my bag, and follow. "Where are you going?"

Rather than head for the shop's front, he exits from the back into the alley leading to the roof. This time, he heads to the street opposite the shop's entrance. It's a quieter block, mainly sporting a row of parked cars. The black one he approaches must be his.

"Get in," he commands before claiming the driver's seat.

"Where are we going?" I ask, hesitating on the curb.

His answer is to slam the driver's side door, leaving me no choice but to open the one nearest me. The interior is black leather, and while I'm not an expert on cars, I can tell that this one is expensive. Very expensive.

A meticulous level of cleanliness alludes to the care of its owner. Or a desire for control—Branden keeps his the same way.

"Get in," Rafe demands, revving the engine.

Finally, I comply. "Fine. Where are we going?"

"Do you want to buy yourself more time?" He shoots me a searching glance I can't decipher, and I remain silent even as he starts to drive.

Eventually, we reach the city's outskirts, where the close-set buildings give way to sparser winding roads. Our final destination makes me do a double take.

"A bus depot?" I question, reading the sign affixed to the front of a nearby building. "What are you—"

"Wait here." He exits the car, slamming the door in his wake. All I can do is stare as he crosses the street to a row of metal bus shelters. They're mostly empty save for a lone woman slumped against a wall of Plexiglass, a duffel at her feet.

Rafe approaches her, reaching into his pocket. A second later, he withdraws what looks like cash, along with something else that triggers a glimmer of recognition—my phone.

The woman accepts both, tucking them into her duffel as Rafe returns to the car.

"What was that about?" I ask as he starts the car and takes off, heading toward the city.

"That?" He chuckles, his eyes glinting mischievously. "That was a fucking reprieve, bunny. How do you think 'Bran' will like Minnesota?"

It takes a second for it to click, just what he's done. I'm startled by the laugh that escapes my lips, but there's more pain mixed into the sound than amusement.

"That won't fool him for long—"

"It's not meant to," Rafe snaps. "But now you have time. Fucking time. So, use it wisely, bunny. Break away from him. He can't control you anymore. Even if it's only for a day, you're free."

How do I choose to spend the first ten minutes of said freedom? Seated beside him, my mind reeling as he drives us back to his shop. He parks in the alley but doesn't leave the car right away. Instead, he sighs, gripping the steering wheel so tightly his knuckles bulge.

"So why lie about him, huh?" he asks, his voice cold. "Did you get off on it? Watching me fucking squirm? Throwing it in my face that you were—" he breaks off and whirls to face me, jabbing his gaze into my own. "That seems to be your fucking favorite game—playing with fire."

"It wasn't like that," I stammer, though honestly, there isn't a better way of phrasing it. I lied to him, and the guilt feels way worse than expected. "I didn't mean—"

"Then what fucking was it?" His voice is deep enough to penetrate my skin and the bone beneath. "Did you like fucking with my head, is that it? By pretending you were fucking your brother. You know how sick that sounds? God, you sure played me like a motherfucker—"

"How do you think it sounds to say out loud that my brother controls my life?" I bite back, startled by my own ferocity. "That he makes me take pictures of myself every night? That he hid a camera in my bedroom? That he haunts me. That he took away the one piece of power I've ever had over him. That he has me *trapped*! How do you think that sounds?"

My own high-pitched voice mockingly holds the answer. It sounds insane. It sounds pathetic.

It sounds like a living nightmare.

"I'm sorry." Rafe brushes my shoulder, but I cringe from his reach. In this confined space, however, there's nowhere to go. Persistent, his fingers slip through my hair, easily finding my chin. "Look at me."

In the end, he has to grip my jaw and compel me to. His eyes gleam in the glow of a nearby streetlight, his face bathed in shadow. The lack of lighting denies him of his usual swagger. Armed with dark irises and an earnest tone, he's harder to write off. Ignore.

"He hurt you." He enunciates every word as if teaching me a foreign language. "I want to hear you say it. Right now. He hurt you, and you don't owe him a damn thing."

"He's my brother," I blurt out instead. "I *do* owe him. And…"

"And what?" Rafe demands, his eyes slits. "And you deserve to have him beat the shit out of you? Track you? I know men with records who aren't that fucking crazy."

"And… I'm afraid of him—" a ragged exhale robs me of breath. Admitting the truth feels comparable to ripping away the veil I've chosen to live under. As a result, I'm naked in the aftermath, at the mercy of his scrutiny.

"Tell me," he says.

"I'm terrified," I hear a stranger with my voice confess. "He hasn't come after me yet, and I don't know what that means. I don't."

When Branden stews, trouble always follows.

"You're afraid," Rafe repeats, his tone softer. "So, what are you going to do about it?"

What could seem like a cruel line of questioning at first, becomes something else the second I see his face. A dare lurks in his stern expression, one that makes me shudder even before he voices it out loud.

"I can help you be ready for him the next time he shows up."

"How?" I croak. "You teach me how to fight? How to shoot a gun? Very funny."

But he doesn't laugh, and as the seconds tick by, I start to remember something Gino insinuated about his father. *Your uncle is one cold son of a bitch, though he has nothing on your daddy. You should know that, though. Aren't you the one who turned his ass in?*

"I'll teach you whatever it takes for you to not be afraid of him," Rafe declares.

The intensity in his voice takes my breath away.

"You're being ridiculous." I can't even face him, so I stare through the windshield instead, watching the orange glow play off the brick siding of the buildings nearby.

"Tell me then," he says, refusing to let the subject drop. "What's your plan? What do you think it will take?"

What will it take to feel safe from Branden?

I'd naïvely thought that finding my voice might do that. Strengthening my writing enough for my own words to speak for me. I thought stating the truth, even as distorted as I could, might help nurture some small, distant part of me brave enough to stand against him.

Weeks later and that hasn't happened.

"I just need to get into the writing program," I insist as dryly as reading a script. "Keep my job. Stay away from him. Nothing else."

"The offer stands," Rafe says while muscling open the door on his end. He mounts the curb, leaving me to scramble after him as he strides ahead for the back door to the shop. Halfway there, he stops short.

"Shit," I hear him hiss as he raises a hand for me to stop. Low, his voice reaches me, barely audible. "Stay here."

CHAPTER FOUR

He inches forward, his posture hunched like a guard dog. The only thing I can make out to explain his unease is the tail end of a bright red car. I've seen it before. Where?

Rafe's already rounding the corner, but I can't shake the instinctive urge in the pit of my soul to move as well—in the opposite direction. *To run. Hide.*

The second I take a step back, Rafe's voice rings out, but directed at someone else. "Uncle. I was—"

"I know what the fuck you were doing," a man replies. I recognize his voice—a guttural baritone that invokes the image of a snarling lion in contrast to Rafe's figurative dragon. "Once again, you were shirking your responsibility. Making me look like a goddamn fool for leaving you in charge at all. A girl was killed in our fucking territory, Rafael. And yet you're off wetting your cock while threats to us mount."

"It's not what it looks like," Rafe counters.

"It's not? I heard what happened here," Shen says. "That you cowered while those thugs sent you a direct warning. Even if this fucking excuse for a hobby is just a game to you, this place is under my territory. Mine."

"Uncle," Rafe starts. "I was going to—"

"You never called for backup," the man says over him. "You never initiated retaliation. I had to find out about it from fucking rumors like it's goddamn amateur hour—" he breaks off. "Come. We need to discuss this. Now. And in the meantime, you can explain why you covered Zhang's tab in full. That son of a bitch doesn't have that kind of money. Did you do it to impress the little whore that works there? Don't look so surprised. Like father like son—easily distracted by a willing cunt—"

"I'm not some boy you can call to heel," Rafe says, his voice gruffer than I've ever heard it. "I told you—confronting Gino head-on is what that son of a bitch wants. He wants to draw us into the open. I thought you wanted to lay low? That petty crime was above you now, Mr. Politician?"

The startled silence from his uncle's end adds a chilling effect to the conversation. Despite not seeing either party's face, I can easily pick up on the shift in the atmosphere— Rafe crossed a glaring red line.

"The cops are on his dick," he continues more softly. "I know it. We need to—"

"We?" His uncle echoes. "You don't decide a damn thing until you get your priorities in order. I may not be able to 'call you to heel,' but I'll give you a choice. I have every intention of keeping *my* hands 'clean,' but you haven't earned the same right."

"What are you saying?" Rafe counters, his alarm apparent by the subtle inflection in his voice.

"I'm saying, either you take a job for me—now. Or I'll extract double Zhang's debt from the little cunt you covered for."

"Job... I thought you were out of the fucking game?"

"I am," Shen insists. "*You're* taking the fucking risk. Or will you do the smart thing, Rafael?"

Silence falls, but I doubt the conversation is anywhere near over. I imagine them facing off, symbolically wrestling over a decision I don't understand in full—but whatever it is, I sense it's momentous. Life or death.

"Where?" Rafe says finally.

"Get in the fucking car," Shen commands. "We'll see how far you're willing to go to prove your loyalty."

Two sets of footsteps advance in my direction but stop short of the alley. I hear a couple car doors open and shut nearby. Minutes later, the red car vanishes from my line of sight.

When I creep from the mouth of the alley, Rafe is gone too, the street deserted.

A job. The way both he and his uncle uttered that word doesn't bring to mind the image of a typical nine-to-five.

But whatever he's doing, it's because of me. That much is clear by his uncle's reference to Mr. Zhang. He's punishing Rafe because of me.

And I have no way of helping. I don't even have anywhere to go. My only option seems to be waiting for him in the alley, or on the roof.

But as a flicker of movement catches the corner of my eye, I realize that neither option may be available. Headlights ignite a block down, belonging to a vehicle I can't make out. It pulls away from the curb, heading toward me at a speed that sends my body lurching into motion. *Run.*

I turn on my heel and start walking, praying that the driver keeps going. I'm being paranoid, overreacting to any little disturbance. Instead, it slows, coming close enough for me to make out the model—a sleek black sedan, far different from Branden's functional cruiser.

The driver lurks behind a tinted window, hidden from view as the car stops. The back door opens, and a figure climbs out. Tall and bulky, he mounts the curb, his dark eyes cutting in my direction.

This time, I don't suppress my first instinct. *Run!*

I take off, careening down the nearest alley—an overreaction I could write off later in a brief moment of embarrassment. Or not. Footsteps ricochet off the walls behind me, creating a dizzying cacophony. As I increase my pace, so do they, even turning a corner after I do.

Following me.

I surge forward, following this back road onto a larger, busier street. Enough pedestrians crowd the sidewalks here for me to blend in. Panting, I slow my stride to match a gaggle of giggling teenage girls and risk looking back. A man staggers from the alley in my wake. His eyes scan the crowd, hunting. Within a heartbeat, they latch onto my position, and he lunges, pushing his way through the throng of people.

With no other choice, I step into the street, dodging the moving traffic. A driver narrowly misses me by inches, but I make it to the other side unscathed. The man, however, is already doing the same, skirting an oncoming truck.

I keep moving, sprinting around the next corner, and I nearly run directly into another person. They grab my wrist automatically, and I react purely on instinct. I don't even realize my free hand is forming a fist until I brandish it.

"Hannah?"

It takes me a second to recognize the man gaping at me. *Liam.* "Are you okay?" he asks. "What the hell happened to you?"

Judging from the way he's eyeing my face, he can clearly make out every detail of my bruises, despite the dark.

"What are you doing here?" I ask. Though when I scan the nearby street, I realize we're not far from the bookstore.

"I just got off," he explains, but his grip on my forearm tightens before I can pull away. "God. What the hell happened—"

"I'm fine," I lie, evading the hand he extends toward my face. "I… I'm just getting off too. I should go."

"I'll walk you," he suggests, looping his arm around my shoulder before I can refuse. "You were at work all day?"

The suspicion in his tone is painfully apparent, but I don't have another lie at the ready. So I nod, avoiding eye contact.

"Huh. Branden didn't come by? He seemed worried about you. You guys get into a fight or something?"

"No. Why?"

"He's been messaging me all day asking if I've seen you," Liam says. He has a cell phone in his free hand, but, as if aware of my gaze, he tucks the device into his pocket.

Was he communicating with Branden?

"It's nothing," I say quickly, forcing a smile. "Just family stuff. You don't need to bother him."

"Family stuff." He smiles in return, but the expression seems strained at the edges.

We're already back on the main street, though I don't spot the man following me. Regardless, I can't shake the feeling that I'm being watched.

Hunted with every step I take.

"I'm not trying to pry or anything," Liam explains. "It's just, he was really worried about you—"

"Hannah!"

That voice… I stiffen, sensing someone approaching behind me. I know without turning around who stands there now. His hand lands over my shoulder, bearing down with increasing brutality until I have to bite back a cry.

"I'll take it from here," Branden says, presumably to Liam. "Thanks for the heads-up."

"Wait." Liam swipes his hand along my jaw, narrowly avoiding the worst of the bruises. "What happened—"

"I've got it," Branden insists. "Thanks."

Liam frowns but backs away. "Okay. Let me know if you need anything."

"Let's go, Hannah." Branden tugs on my shoulder, but I don't move, digging my heels into the pavement. "You don't want to make a scene," he warns against my neck. "All I want to do is talk—" his nails bite down with renewed strength, and he tugs, positioning himself beside me so that Liam can't catch my pained gasp.

"You're hurting me," I croak.

"Good," he counters, muscling me further down the block and fully out of earshot. "Do you have any fucking idea what you've put me through? Do you? It's like you're a selfish little brat all over again."

There's no one else on this street, apparently a quiet residential roadway. Lights in various windows allude to populated homes, their occupants within earshot of a scream.

But I can't seem to voice one.

If I'm a selfish little brat again, then he's the same towering figure who's dominated my memories for as long as I can remember.

But I don't even recognize him now. And despite everything he's done, there are some actions I've never considered him capable of.

"You watched me," I say in a hoarse whisper, the loudest sound I seem capable of producing. "You spied on me, Bran. You saw me—"

"I've protected you," he hisses, nudging me forward. "I still am. Rafe Wei-Shen? Do you have any idea what that fucker is capable of? What he's done?"

His hissed tone carries far too much rage.

"Why don't you ask around? I hear you're not even the first girl he's seduced. *Or* manipulated into doing his dirty work, but it's not even you he's interested in—"

"And what about you?" I ask, finally turning to face him directly. "Who have you 'manipulated'? Faith Wen?"

Surprise visibly crosses his face, but it goes far beyond typical shock. I've only witnessed his eyes narrow like this a handful of times. He's afraid. "What are you talk—"

"You know what I'm talking about, Bran!" I wrench away, causing his nails to gouge at my arm in the process. Rather than run, it's like my body is controlled by someone else. Someone reckless, who makes me meet his gaze head-on.

I don't recognize the man staring back.

He's not in uniform, and his mussed hair proves Liam's story. He's been out for hours, looking for me. Despite his best attempts, his neutral expression fails to convince me. Again, his eyes give him away, flashing and cold, a hard reflective green. In his gaze, I see myself staring back, every bit as gaping and stupid as the bunny Rafe implies I am.

But no more.

"I found the hair clip," I rasp.

"Hair clip?" He sounds so convincing I almost fall for it. But his supposed confusion never reaches his eyes—if anything, they remain frozen. Ice-cold.

"It's silver, in the shape of a butterfly," I explain. "I found it in a box of my things, but it isn't mine."

"What makes you think I put it there?" he demands, raising an eyebrow. "It probably is one of yours. You just forgot you had it, and you're so paranoid about making me the bad guy you'll jump to any conclusion you can."

"So, you don't know Faith?" I ask him. "She was found dead the other day. She waited on us at the restaurant. She was seeing a police officer, and—"

"Who told you all of this?" Branden interjects harshly. "Honestly, Hannah, you sound ridiculous."

"Just tell me you didn't do it," I whisper, and I'm surprised by just how earnest I sound. Desperate. "Tell me, Bran. Tell me you didn't."

"Do what?" he hisses, advancing a step, his hands in fists. "Catch you fucking a criminal? Lie to our parents when you disappear for days, Hannah? Think you were on your way to only God knows where? If Liam didn't spot you when he did—" he exhales with a gruff sound akin to a growl. "Why don't you ask your boyfriend about who's been planting shit on you? You really have no idea what he's capable of. Do you? Don't tell me you're dumb enough to think he'd be interested in you for no reason. To him, you're just leverage. Don't believe me?"

A tendril of doubt sneaks into my brain. After all, Rafe was the one who moved my things from my apartment in the first place. He had more than enough opportunity to hide something in a seemingly random box of trinkets.

But...

"Something else was missing from my things too," I say, watching Branden for any hint of a reaction. "A gold bracelet. Does that ring a bell?"

"Jesus Christ, Hannah! Why are you trying to provoke me? Do you want me to fuck up again, huh? Like what you made me do the last time."

I stiffen at the reminder.

Last time.

A fit of violence triggered because of me.

Everything he does is *always* because of me, even now. I'm the reason for the flush of red creeping across his neck, visible even in the dark. I'm the reason why his hands are twitching as if he's having to physically stop himself from striking me again. I'm the reason for his lack of control.

"Answer me!"

"Did you hurt that girl?" I ask instead. God, I can barely get the words out.

But they ring hollow. Laughing, he rolls his eyes. "What girl? Or is this just another game, Hannah? How you avoid blame. There's always another girl, isn't there? Like Lexi?" He scoffs when I recoil. "Ah, but you wouldn't want to use that memory against me, Hannah? When it was your fault that she died. You wouldn't be trying to delude yourself into thinking otherwise, would you? Enough!" He snaps his fingers. "Come home—"

"You killed her." My voice breaks, robbing the accusation of any grit. Regardless, I think it's the first time I've ever said those words out loud.

Am I referring to Faith? Or Lexi?

I don't even know anymore.

Rather than react in anger, Branden just keeps laughing. "Hannah, stop it. You know how crazy you sound?"

He advances another step, and I nearly trip in my rush to put distance between us.

"Don't touch me—"

"Come home," he snarls. "Now. While Dad remains clueless about how much of a little whore you really are. While he's still paying for your fucking, stupid school. But will he if he knows the truth, Hannah?"

I blink in confusion. "The truth?"

His smile turns feral—I've taken his bait. "That you're out here selling sex tapes on the internet while he funds your education? Or your school... Do you think that liberal fucking college would like to know one of their students is an online video star?"

I can feel the blood drain from my face as I stop dead in my tracks. "You didn't..."

"I will," he says coldly. "Unless you come with me now. I love you, Hannah, but if you want to act like a whore, I will treat you like one. Now come home—"

"Why?" I demand, evading his grasping hand. "Why are you doing this?"

"Because I love you," he insists. "I do. So, make your choice right now. Come home with me, or learn the hard way— I'm the only one you can ever trust."

He reaches for me again, but I shirk his grasp. Again. Again. Eventually, several feet of space separate us, but he just watches me, stunned.

"Hannah—"

"I could still tell," I hear myself say in that stranger's broken tone. "Daddy. The police. Everyone."

"Tell them what?"

My heart despairs at the answer. One that's haunted me for the past ten years. "That you were never worth the benefit of the doubt."

"You little bitch... If you think I'm the liar, then where is your proof, huh?" He eyes my bag, his nostrils flaring. "Where is it?"

When he comes for me this time, I turn on my heel and run.

"Hannah!" His voice chases me as I dart between two parked cars and cross the street. He's on my heels. His heavy pants lash at the air, his footsteps slamming against the pavement—but with every step I gain, they grow distant, until only his shouts can reach me.

"I'll give you until tomorrow night, Hannah. One fucking night! You come to me when you're ready to learn your lesson, or the world will learn the truth about *you*—you were always just a lying little whore!"

Tears lash at my cheeks as I keep moving, darting from alley to alley and street to street. Eventually, I no longer recognize my surroundings, and only fear keeps me going, driving me further into an increasingly industrial area where warehouses and office buildings take up most of the real estate.

I'm too busy replaying Branden's threat to even care that I'm lost. Would he truly do that? Post whatever he recorded on the internet. Make it seem like I did it. Lie. Cheat. All to keep me under his thumb?

The answer sickens me to my stomach—he would. He will.

And I'm powerless to do a damn thing to stop him.

A sudden smattering of noise draws my attention, and I finally falter. At a glance, the street I'm on is deserted, but up ahead, I spot a building that may have been my destination all along—a warehouse near the wharf.

A battered door serves as the entrance, but it's unlocked. Musty air tickles my nostrils as I feel through the dark until I find a hallway leading into a larger space. The first time I came here, a light had illuminated much of the enclosed area ahead, but now it's pitch-black.

Something clatters as I stumble against it. I forge ahead until my hand meets a surface I assume to be a wall, and I gladly sink to the floor, bracing my back against it.

I keep as still as I can, listening for any other sound. If Branden is still on my trail, enclosing myself in here is a stupid course of action, but it's one that I can't seem to talk myself out of. Maybe because a persistent warning is echoing in my mind on repeat. *You get there, and you wait for me.*

I should still be running. Fighting. Or better yet, getting ahold of my parents somehow and telling them the truth—about everything.

A laugh escapes me, as if even my body knows what my brain can't face. I won't. I've spent too many years resisting those very actions—too many years obscuring the truth.

And as a result, no one would believe me. Hell, even I wouldn't.

But Rafe did, a part of me whispers. He believed me without question, displaying a disgust for my circumstances that I've never had the energy to feel myself.

Is it genuine? Parsing over his responses, I can't tell. For someone who claims to be so honest, he's more guarded than not, displaying his real emotions only through layers at a time. And one fact remains painfully clear—I hardly know anything about him.

His true profession. His history with his uncle. His past.

Branden could be right. Rafe could have planted Faith's hair clip. A good sister would want to believe as much.

Do I?

Rather than mull over the answer, I lean back against the wall, settling into the strange, darkened space. The building must be old, given the various creaking, cracking noises that form a backdrop to my own harsh breathing.

But soon, another noise joins the quiet cacophony—heavy, cautious footsteps.

CHAPTER FIVE

"Hannah?"

I tense at the sound of my name before my body registers the cadence of the voice speaking it.

"I'm here," I croak, feeling along the floor as I stand.

An overhead light switches on, bathing the room in an orange glow—as well as revealing the pile of chaos I've left in my wake. I'm standing on a stack of overturned documents, marred by a muddy footprint that looks suspiciously like it might belong to my sandal. Out of guilt, I shuffle the pages together and attempt to return them to the nearest table.

The topmost one catches my eye as I try to shove it inside a folder. It's a slip of paper with the city police emblem emblazoned across the top. Beneath that is a list of what seems to be names. Several of them have been crudely circled in red ink.

One, in particular, catches my eye, halfway down the page —Branden Dewitt.

"Hannah?" Rafe stands a few feet away, his back to me. "Where are you?"

I snatch the list, tucking it into my bag. "I'm over here!" I approach him slowly, sensing even before I come close that something is horribly wrong. "Rafe…"

He's leaning to one side, heavily favoring that leg. His left hand clutches at his chest, and a telltale smell tickles my nostrils, growing more potent by the second.

"You're bleeding," I say, scanning his frame for any other signs of injury—which I find in a spattered trail of blood leading from the hall, tracking his entry. "What happened?"

Groaning, he hobbles to a sturdy table nearby and braces his hands over it. "Give me a hand," he demands, his voice hoarse. "Black case in the corner."

With the words barely out of his mouth, he slumps forward, knocking the table off balance.

I lurch toward him. "Rafe—"

"Just get the fucking case," he grates, lifting a hand to ward me off. "Please…"

I whirl on my heel, struggling to follow his instructions. The room is a maze of stray materials. Stacks of canvases. Boxes piled high with random equipment. Stray slabs of plywood lean against the wall, obscuring a shelf in a far corner. On it, I find a black leather construct resembling a briefcase.

I bring it to Rafe, setting it beside him.

"You don't look good," I rasp. He's shaking, barely capable of supporting himself on trembling hands. Still, he risks that precarious balance to grab the case, dragging it toward him. For all the effort, he fumbles with the latch. "Fuck—"

"I'll do it." I unlatch the top of the case, opening it to reveal a sight that takes my breath away. Fear constricts my throat, and all I seem capable of doing is whispering, "Rafe…"

"Don't," he warns before overturning the case entirely, allowing the contents to spill out onto the table's surface. Money. Stacks and stacks of crisp bills, each secured with a rubber band. There have to be hundreds. Thousands…

But the amount pales in comparison to what falls amid the scattered stacks, its shape unmistakable—a gun.

Rafe grabs for it first, tucking it into his pocket. When he reaches for a stack of cash next, droplets of blood drip from his fingers, staining a handful of bills. "Damn it." He forms a fist instead, cocking his head in my direction. "I need you to grab it."

I barely hear him. More blood is dripping from his chin, flowing from his split lip. Fresh bruising around his eye alludes to yet another blow. From one of Gino's goons? From his uncle?

"Did you hear me? Hey, bunny!" He snaps his fingers beneath my nose, but he's so weak they barely make a sound. Scarlet streaks the tips of them, painting a blazing path up his wrist…

Finally, I notice the gash slicing through the flesh of his left arm.

I snatch at his sleeve in alarm. "What the hell happened to you?"

"It doesn't fucking matter. Listen to me!" He slams his hand over the table so hard I swear he dents the wood. However, the act drains him, and I lurch forward to grab his shoulder before he can pitch over entirely. His eyes flit up to mine, and I swallow hard at the agony I find in them. Along with anger. Volatile, infectious rage.

"We need to move," he says, gasping with the effort. "Now—"

"You can barely stand up," I hiss.

He shrugs to throw me off, but he's so weak, he winds up swaying without the support. So he jerks his chin toward the stack of bills instead. "Grab the fucking money. Put it in your purse. Do it. Now." Something in my expression makes him sigh. "Please."

I don't know why that single word affects me—his tone. Maybe the aftermath of confronting Branden has robbed me of the ability to think for myself longer than a few minutes at a time. I grab a stack of bills without realizing it.

Then another—but at the back of my mind gnaws this irrational sense of hurt. Betrayal.

He's making me do this but won't tell me why. So much for freedom.

"That's enough," he says when I've grabbed four stacks of bills. "Put the rest back. Good. Now… I need you to come with me."

He pulls away from the table and staggers a few steps toward the exit. He doesn't even make it halfway before he careens into a pile of canvas. A volley of curses erupts from him as they—and him along with them—crash to the floor.

Rushing to him, I hook my arm around his shoulders, hauling him to his feet. I spot a metal folding chair nearby, and I practically drag him to it, making him sit. My eyes latch onto the way he's still clutching at his side, and I seize the hem of his shirt, wrenching it up despite his attempts to stop me.

"Don't—"

"Oh my God…" I drop to my knees to get a better look. Where there was once unblemished skin, mottled bruising paints his ribcage in a medley of purples. He must have been struck by something—heavy enough to leave a cylindrical area the width of his chest. A bat? A larger weapon?

"God, Rafe. You could have internal damage." I can't stop myself from brushing my hand along his ribcage, and he nearly jumps off the chair.

"Fuck!"

"What happened?" My voice rings out stronger as I rise to my feet. "Tell me, or I'm leaving. I mean it—"

"I need you." He looks me dead in my eyes, leaving no doubt that he means every word. "I need you, bunny. Don't ask questions. Not now. I'll explain everything later, but for now… You've gotta trust me."

"No." I back away and nearly trip over an array of scattered pens that must have fallen from the table. "You don't have the right to ask me to do that. You don't!"

He wrestles his shirt into place, and I can tell from how unfocused his gaze becomes that he's barely on the verge of coherence. In essence, he's miles away, still running from whatever drove him here.

Lowering my voice, I try to reason with him. "You need a hospital—"

"If I don't do this, we're both dead." He says it so plainly that I continue to talk over him without registering the depth of his words at first.

"An ambulance. You could be bleeding internally… What are you talking about?"

He grits his teeth in determination as he grips the end of the chair. The damn thing nearly topples as he rises to his feet.

"Trust me." He extends a hand marred by blood, and only God knows what else. It's so repulsive I recoil—or I start to.

The second I flinch, his gaze locks me in place, paralyzing in its raw intensity.

I can read his emotions in every nuanced quirk from his lips, pursed and tight, to his brow furrowed with concentration. As well as the feeling making him sway to stay upright—fear.

That sole observation affects me like nothing else. Robotic steps propel me forward, and my hand extends without input from my brain, my fingers entwining with his. He tugs me to his side, utilizing my body as a makeshift cane.

"I need to get to my car," he grates through his teeth. "Come on."

We head for the exit surprisingly fast, but every few seconds, his eyes dart toward the shadows. Whatever he sees —or doesn't—has him tightening his grip, urging me into the closest speed he can come to an outright run. Which is little more than a hobbling walk.

"This way." Once we reach his car, he wrenches open the driver's side door, but rather than claim it for himself, he nudges me closer. "Can you drive?"

"Yes, but I haven't in years," I admit. And this modern dashboard looks far different from the hand-me-down family car I practiced with back in PA. "But—"

"Do it. Please." Without giving me the chance to respond, he limps around to the passenger's side, clinging to the car for balance. "We need to move." He shoots another wary glance over his shoulder, and unease drives me inside despite my instincts warning me to jump right back out.

I can't do this—get dragged into whatever this is. But then Rafe slumps onto the seat beside me, and one look at his face breaks my resolve. I've never seen him like this. His hands shaking, his eyes unfocused with pain. For once, there's no bravado.

"Please."

Defeated, I turn my attention to the modern console. "Where are the keys? And where are we going?"

He strikes a button on the dashboard, and the engine roars to life. "Just drive," he commands. "I'll tell you where to go."

Where winds up being an area roughly ten miles away, following the waterline north. I can't tell if we're still within the city limits, though the only buildings in sight are a few scattered warehouses. The road itself is sparsely populated—which is a blessing in disguise, considering I'm going roughly fifty miles below the speed limit.

"Damn, bunny," Rafe chokes out, the first thing he's said other than a few grunted directions. "My grandmother drives faster than this."

"Then maybe you should call her." God, I don't recognize myself anymore—a stranger apart from the fearful figure who cowered in Branden's shadow. This Hannah is angry. Seething. And worried.

For *him.*

All I can do is pour my energy into driving, recalling the few skills I learned before moving to the city. I won't admit it out loud, but it's a miracle we've made it this far.

"Turn here," Rafe demands, indicating a shallow, gnarled road that looks unwelcoming at best. "Trust me," he prods, sensing my hesitation. "But I won't lie to you, bunny. Shit's about to get real. Now park."

I slam my foot on the brake so suddenly, Rafe grips the dashboard to keep from flying out of his seat.

"Fuck," he hisses, clutching at his side. "Now... Do you still have the money?"

"Y-Yes." I scramble for my bag, which I find tucked beneath the seat.

"Good. Now I need you to take it over to that building—" he indicates a massive industrial complex that looks to be about several years past its prime. Some of the windows are broken, the interior darkened, and plenty of rust is visible in the dim illumination provided by a streetlight. "You'll find an old dumpster beside it," he tells me. "Open the sliding door. Put the money in, and whatever is inside, you take it and run the fuck back. I'd do it myself, but we gotta do this quick."

His tone alarms me more than reassures. "What are you—"

"I'll have your back," he says over me. "Trust me, I won't let anything happen to you. But you've gotta do this. Now."

He leans over me to wrench open my door.

"Go," he snarls.

I move entirely out of reflex, stumbling to my feet. It's quiet here. Every step echoes, amplified until it sounds like a million other people follow in my wake. Armed with only his money, I've never felt more exposed.

"Go," Rafe prompts from the window. "You won't be on your own. I've got you."

He's got you, a part of me hisses. *As a puppet. A fool. Just like Branden.*

But I rightfully ran away from that monster. This one? I blindly follow into the shadows, as stupidly as the bunny he mocks me for being.

Find a dumpster, he said.

The only one I find lurks behind the nearest building. From here, the car is hidden from view, and yawning shadows dance over a desolate pavement littered with broken glass and growing weeds.

The dumpster itself is rusted through in places, but sure enough, the door that, were it in use, would allow trash to be thrown through it opens when I tug on the handle. The interior has been modified—a wooden ledge provides a place to set the bills on, and resting in the space already is another case. As I reach for it, a flicker of movement catches my eye. I barely manage to pivot as a hand reaches out from nowhere.

"Who the fuck are you?" a man demands. A bittersweet stench tinges his breath. Alcohol? He's bulky, his face obscured by shadow, but I instantly recognize the object in his grasp—a knife. "I said who the fuck are you—"

"We're here for the drop," someone declares from behind me. "She left the money. We'll take what we're owed and then go."

"So, you *did* show, after all, you dumb son of a bitch," the man says, laughing. "I hear your uncle whipped your ass good. But here you are, doing his bidding like a good doggie."

"Leave." Rafe's voice touches on a note so deep my entire body vibrates in response. "Take the fucking money and go."

"You're in trouble from what I hear, mutt," the man snarls. "Shen's not too happy with you, is he? You must have pissed him off good for him to use you as an errand boy. But he gave you the wrong information. This shipment isn't for you—"

"What the hell are you talking about?" Rafe demands.

The man steps forward, and a stream of orange light illuminates his gaunt features. "I'm saying, you got bad information, mongrel. Now get the fuck out of here." He deliberately reaches for his pocket, but suddenly goes stiff as I sense Rafe step forward.

"Don't even think about it," he growls.

"Like you have what it takes," the man says with a chuckle, but he raises his hands in surrender.

Rafe's shadow thrown over the ground gives me an inkling as to why. He stands at my shoulder, a slender object held between his fingers.

"You think you scare me?" The man laughs. "Your own uncle doesn't even keep you in the loop. You have no idea, do you? The game he's been playing at your expense? Setting you up to take his fall like the little patsy you are—"

"I said go."

"You really want to fuck around like this, Rafael? Steal from me?" The man doesn't move for so long I lose feeling in my clenched hands. Finally, he backs away, his knife still raised. "You'll pay for this."

"Come on." Reaching past me, Rafe snatches the case, tucking it under his arm. His hand latches onto my forearm next, imparting a strength that keeps the fear at bay long enough to navigate the ruined buildings.

We return to the car surprisingly fast, but when I finally see his face, it's apparent just how much effort maintaining the façade cost him. He's pale enough to glow in the dark, swaying on his feet.

"Just drive," he chokes out before collapsing onto the passenger's seat. "Drive…"

But he never drops the gun. If anything, his grip on it tightens as if any second, he expects to use it.

And he's more than willing to do so.

CHAPTER SIX

"You're pissed," Rafe declares. In a stark contrast to his fearsome display near the dumpster, he's lying flat on his couch, his head propped on an armrest.

He's stripped his shirt revealing the full extent of his injuries. A makeshift towel bandage staunches most of the bleeding from his arm, but the bruising on his chest worsens by the second. With every inhale, he winces, but somehow manages to sport a guilty frown. "I'm sorry—"

"You used me." It isn't until I hear my own voice that I realize just how angry I am. Hurt. Betrayed. Humiliated.

Of course, he used you, a part of me hisses. *You made it so easy for him to.*

"I did," he bluntly admits. "And you helped me anyway. I owe ya again, bunny. I mean that."

One look at him, and I think he's telling the truth. He looks so tired. Exhausted.

But I stamp out any pity I may feel and cross my arms, shifting my weight in the direction of the door. Where I'd go, I have no idea. Just away. Somewhere far away from all of it.

"You owe me," I parrot with a scoff. "Good. Well, you can start by telling me the truth. No 'what do you think it is, bunny?' stuff. You be honest with me now, or I'm leaving. What the hell was that?"

"That..." He chokes out another sigh. "I believe the technical term is 'a drug deal,' but you can be creative about it if you want."

"A drug deal?" I brace myself against the nearest wall, but it doesn't feel anywhere near sturdy enough to support me.

"More or less," he says. His eyes meet mine, devoid of any mocking, and I know deep down, he isn't lying. "It might be slightly melodramatic to say it was life or death too, but I'm not far off."

"Who hurt you?" I ask, though I figure a part of me already knows the answer.

"That..." He groans, clutching his side as he starts to sit upright. "Well, I've gotta keep some secrets close to the vest, bunny—"

"No!" My hands find my hips, and I'm seconds away from stomping my foot in anger. "No more secrets. You tell me everything now, or I'm leaving. And while we're at it—" I reach into my bag and withdraw the list of names, brandishing it in his direction. "You tell me about this."

His expression remains blank, devoid of shock, or alarm. "And where are you going to go?" He doesn't sound threatening, just curious.

And it's a darn good question. Where the hell am I going to go with my face bruised to hell and back, no car and no money?

Though, his keys are still in my hand—a fact he only seems to realize as I lift them and consider doing the obvious.

"Anywhere is better than staying with a liar."

"Fine." Groaning, he braces himself against the back of the couch. "I fucked up bad. To make up for it, I needed to do a job for Shen, or he'd bring hell down on both of us. Trust me, this was the lesser of two evils. I bought us time. As for the list. I was working my way through the cops that patrol this area trying to find Faith's 'DW.'" He cracks a tired grin that doesn't reach his eyes. "Funnily enough, there aren't many officers with a first name that starts with D and last name starting with W. Go fucking figure."

I can't hide the way my shoulders slump in relief. He sounds honest—which means he hasn't zoned in on Branden yet. Or at least, I can't tell from his pained expression if he has.

"So, what is in the case?" I ask, crossing my arms.

His eyes dart to the object in question, now resting beside the door. In the glow of a hanging lightbulb, it looks more intimidating than ever, containing only God knows what.

"You know," I say hoarsely, "you bitched at me for lack of detail, but you suck at it."

"Fine. You want to know the truth?" Some of the cockiness deflates from his demeanor. "I'm in deep with the family business, rabbit. If I didn't toe the line, my uncle threatened to drag you into my mess and have you work off what I owed. Every penny, and I can tell you for a fact that it wouldn't be in a fucking shop. He's a petty bastard with a nasty streak, and I've already pissed him off one too many times. I can't fight him on even footing. All I can do is shut him up for as long as I can by toeing the line. How is that for detail?"

His face conveys so much frustration and rage that I'm infected by both.

"Driving a getaway car wasn't ideal," he adds, "but trust me, it's a better deal than what he had in mind."

Work off...

I let the wall support most of my weight as I sink to the floor, crossing my legs beneath me. "Why me?"

He shrugs, wincing with the effort. "You were around, and I was dumb enough to think he wasn't fucking watching my every move. Don't take it personally. He's always been a controlling cunt."

He glowers at the ceiling, and I can't ignore the part of me that aches in sympathy.

I recognize that look. It's the same one I see the few times I'm brave enough to look in a mirror.

"He hurt you," I deduce. He doesn't react, but I sense it's the truth. "Is that what he does to keep you working for him? Hurt you. Make you commit crimes at his say so?"

"He's getting out of the game," he says tiredly. "It's only until I can break away on my own."

"So, now what?"

"I bought us time," he snaps, his gaze on his hands, bruised and streaked with blood. One by one, he curls a fist, his frown determined. "That's what."

Discomfort congeals in the pit of my stomach, growing with every tidbit of information I wring from him.

But I can't resist asking for more. "What kind of drugs?"

"Bad drugs, bunny. The kind that goes up your nose or into a vein. Shen's been out of the game for years due to the risk —at least directly. He's been focusing on 'legal' revenue, buying up property and shit. Trying to stay clean for a pivot into politics, I guess. The drugs are petty change to him now. He just made me get my hands dirty to prove a point."

What kind of point takes this kind of risk to prove?

"How much money did you give up?" I ask him not out of curiosity—but a twisted need to keep this conversation going. As long as he's still talking, I don't have to process this. Not yet.

He wrinkles his sore lip, pondering the question. "A fucking lot of money."

"Money that you get by selling and buying drugs? And shaking down shop owners," I add, picturing his interactions with Mr. Zhang. "Is this what you do? Sell cocaine or heroin—" the two most dangerous drugs I know of, "and then shake down old men to stay 'legal'?"

He doesn't shy from my accusing gaze. "Bunny, where the hell do you think Zhang's debt comes from?"

"What... I..." Shock renders me speechless.

"The old man's had a problem for years, between that and gambling. That store of his has kept him afloat, but he's racked up more on his tab than you would think. But I let it slide," he adds, staring beyond me. "I thought I could make up the deficit on my own, but..."

"For me," I croak, filling in the blanks of what he doesn't say. "You let it slide because of me."

Silent, he glowers into space, but he lost his grip on the towel in the course of the conversation, letting his arm bleed freely again.

Cautiously, I stand and approach him, eyeing the wound. "He did this to you?" Up close, the viciousness of the injury is on full display. I can't imagine a family member doing this to his own nephew—though I'm not one to talk.

Given their shape, his injuries could be caused by a fist. A shoe. His body striking something hard enough to slice into his arm. Brutal, grueling punishment.

"Don't worry about it," he says, dismissing me with a wave of his good hand.

I don't move. "You might need stitches."

"I might." He cocks his head toward me and lets his hand fall. "You up for it, Florence Nightheart?"

"Nightingale," I correct through a lump in my throat. Sinking down beside him, I wad up the towel and press it against the gash, applying pressure despite his hisses of agony. "I have to stop the bleeding," I explain as he groans. "I'm not even pressing that hard."

"I'll let you in on a secret, bunny," he says, his voice tight. "I fucking hate pain. Hate it. Call me a pussy, but it is what it is."

"Your ribs could be broken," I point out, alarmed by the discoloration over his chest. Not to mention what might happen if the wound on his arm severed an artery. "Why do it? Work for him?" I ask without taking my eyes off the bloodstained towel. "You have money. You have your shop. You have your talent. Or is it all just a front?" I'm surprised by the sheer amount of anger leaching into my tone.

"Why?" He turns his gaze to the ceiling, frowning as if he never considered the question before now. Whatever conclusion he comes to makes him exhale dejectedly. "It's not that simple."

"Explain it then," I snap. "In 'pretty words.' Why?"

"I don't know… Call it genetics."

I pause in my ministrations. "What do you mean?"

"My father ran shit for him," he admits, wincing in pain. "Drugs. Getaway driving. Worse. You name it, I'm sure he did it all for good old uncle Shen. When he tried to get out? Shen cut him off, and—big surprise—the bastard, couldn't hold a stable job. He left my mother to come crawling back to his brother on her hands and knees just to get by."

"So what?" I ask softly. "You follow in his footsteps?"

His eyes blaze, warning I've crossed a line. "What else am I going to fucking do?"

"What you want," I suggest.

He scoffs. "Like you're the expert on that subject?"

But I'm not him. Brave and powerful, armed with an undeniable talent.

"I bet you could make more doing tattoos," I add, observing the flames licking down the length of the arm I'm treating. "You know, *legally*?"

"Is that a dare, bunny?"

I purse my lips, making up my mind on the spot. "You said you owe me? Well, that's how you'll pay me back."

"I thought you were supposed to be working for *me*?" His lip quirks into a genuine smile I'm unprepared for. Crooked and faint, it softens him despite the blood and bruises. He could be a different person—at least until he grits his teeth, closing up once more. "Unless you want to find another way to pay me back?"

Innuendo seeps from his tone. Hunting for a distraction, I peel back the towel, satisfied by the wound's depth once most of the blood is wiped away. "Your arm has stopped bleeding," I deduce, rearing back to meet his gaze. "You'll live. I guess you don't need stitches after all—"

"Shit, your neck." He lashes out, tugging aside the neckline of my shirt. I don't even notice at first what has him so upset—reddened skin quickly turning purple, marred by tiny imprints left by raking nails.

"I know that fucker at the warehouse didn't touch you," he says, scanning my face like a shark catching a whiff of blood. "Your turn for honesty, bunny. What the fuck happened?"

"He found me," I confess, tugging the collar back into place. I don't feel any pain, but Rafe is persistent, running his fingers along my throat.

"Fuck… Why didn't you come here—"

"The door was locked."

He growls and practically tugs me onto the couch beside him. My shirt is off in seconds, his hands spanning my back in its place. "What the fuck did he do?"

"Nothing, but…"

The words won't come, too twisted to voice out loud. His threat. His ultimatum. The fact that despite his deadline looming over my head, the prospect of going back feels as viable an option as learning how to breathe underwater. Impossible.

"He threatened you, didn't he?" Rafe deduces. His fingers slip through my hair and find my chin, urging me to face him. "That motherfucker. What did he want? For you to come back?"

I nod.

"But that's not all," he suspects as though reading my mind. His fingers part through my hair and form a fist, using the handful to tug me further against him. This way, his mouth has easier access to my ear, and his lips brush the lobe, imparting a taste of his heat. "He did something. Said something he knew would make you consider hopping right back to him, scared."

He waits for a reaction, but all I do is go limp, resting my weight against his uninjured side.

"I don't want to think about him," I confess. "Call it what you want. You hate pain, and I—"

"You hate facing him," he says with a dry chuckle. "I'll call that what it is, bunny—you're human. But if you get to make little demands, then so do I."

His expression is carefully blank, leaving me no clue as to his intentions. "What kind of demands?"

He takes my hand in his, lacing our fingers together before lifting them both for inspection. In a way, we almost resemble some twisted representation of a flame—a golden core with glimpses of ivory peeking through.

"You want me to make some money 'legally'?" He makes the idea sound like a cross between outrageous and amusing. "Fine. But in the meantime, I want you to tell me everything. Everything he's done to you from the very beginning. Your words. Your way. I want you to write it. Every last fucking thing."

He manipulates our fingers, encasing mine within his. "That sounds like a boring story," I say.

"*Your* story," he counters. "Give it to me. That's what I want."

"Why?"

He nestles against the back of the couch, making himself more comfortable. "I told you the first time we met—I want to know what goes on behind those bunny eyes."

More specifically—*I want to know what makes a little rabbit like you so damn hard she doesn't flinch when a man presses a knife to her throat.*

"Fine," I concede. "But I still think you'll find it boring."

"Trust me, bunny." His good arm crosses my chest, locking me to his side. "I could use a little boring in my life right about now."

He sounds so genuinely eager it unnerves me.

A man begging for some hint of boring normalcy.

While I'm running from it.

CHAPTER SEVEN

It's starting to become normal, waking up to the scent of coconut, wrapped in warmth. Like this, I can forget everything else. At least until a heavy body stirs beneath me.

"You're late," someone commands against my ear, his voice gruff with sleep. "I expect my employees to be on the floor by nine a.m. sharp. I should dock your pay. How are you going to convince me not to?"

I open my eyes, stretching out my sore limbs. Gray daylight paints the room in hues of silver, giving everything an ethereal glow. The warmth cocooning my body only enhances the serene mood. I feel a childish desire never to move from this spot.

Going off Rafe's relaxed expression, I think he feels the same —if only my hip wasn't resting directly over a particular part of his anatomy.

"Even unconscious, you're a cock-tease," he remarks, his gaze heavy-lidded. "You can't even have mercy on an injured man?"

I roll off of him, observing the rest of the apartment. While we slept, reality didn't recede an inch—his blood paints a trail across the floor, and that infamous case is still in the entryway. I toy with the idea of seeing its contents for myself. Facing the truth might brand the harsh reality into my skull—this man is dangerous—a criminal.

As if sensing my train of thought, he runs his hand down the middle of my back, contradicting the hard image of him I should maintain. "We're starting over," he declares. "I'm a new man, bunny. On the up and up, remember? I'm making money the legal way. After last night... Don't hold that shit against me, deal?"

I stand rather than answer, approaching one of the windows. The street below is mostly empty apart from the average passing car, but no police cruisers—for now. Still, I'm not comforted.

Branden's deadline rings loud and clear inside my head— *But will he if he knows the truth, Hannah? That you're out here selling sex tapes on the internet while he funds your education? Or your school...*

"You okay?" Rafe demands from behind me. I turn to find him on his feet, grasping an armrest.

"Are you?" I toss back. Some of his color has returned, but his chest looks even worse. I'd be surprised if his ribs aren't broken. The pattern of bruising makes it clear what may have caused the injuries, though. The unmistakable imprint of the sole of a shoe. Or a boot. "God, Rafe," I whisper in horror. "Maybe you should go to the hospital—"

"I'm fine," he snaps. To prove it, he staggers into the hallway, moving with the speed and gait of a seventy-year-old man.

I follow him into the bedroom, where he makes a show of fishing a clean pair of clothing from his wardrobe. Only to howl in pain the second he tries to strip his bloodstained pants.

"Son of a bitch!"

"Let me." I cross to him, dropping to my knees.

If I weren't already aware of how this position may look, his low, agonized grunt would reinforce the awkwardness plenty.

"Damn," he rasps.

I look up to find his lower lip seized between his teeth. "If I knew that getting fucked up was one way to get you on your knees, I would have gotten my ass kicked sooner." His voice is too husky to entirely be joking, his mouth twisted in a grimace most men might sport when having to choose between life and death.

I don't know what possesses me to run my fingers down the length of his inner thigh. He groans, his head shooting back. Then he sighs.

"Not nice. Sadly, I'm gonna have to take a rain check," he says. "But damn, do I intend to make it worth your while when I can move without wanting to cough up blood."

I shiver at the promise, but when he winces in actual agony, my brain shifts gears. I gingerly ease his jeans down his legs and help him step into a fresh pair. When I grab a shirt for him next, however, he scoffs and lumbers into the hallway with his chest bare.

"Give me a few minutes," he warns near the bathroom door. "If I scream, I have not learned how to piss one-handed. I've got a lot to work with when it comes to aiming."

I roll my eyes and grab a fresh skirt from my pile in the hallway. After stripping my soiled shirt, I find myself pulling on the one he discarded—a gray graphic tee with a local sandwich shop's logo on the front. When he staggers from the bathroom a few minutes later, I catch sight of my reflection in the mirror behind him.

God, I have to blink a few times to recognize this strange, different Hannah. She's a mess. Wide-eyed. Dazed. Visible bruises mar the flesh near my right eye, and my jaw is a colorful array of browns and purples.

My collarbone draws most of my attention, however. Tiny marks stand out against the flesh there, left by nipping teeth. Days later, they've settled into a deep burgundy reminiscent of a certain dragon tattoo. I finger one, trying to decipher my reaction. It would be wrong to call them beautiful. Logically, I think they should disturb me just as much as the state of my face does.

I can't even begin to fathom why they don't.

"Come on," Rafe calls from the living room. "I wasn't kidding when I said we were running late. If I'm supposed to be a new and improved motherfucker, earning money through legal means, then I need a shop to work out of, don't I?"

That question apparently ends in him limping down the stairs. He enters the front room and thumbs through an arrangement of flyers tucked beneath the counter.

"Where the hell did I put that fucking hardware brochure?" he mutters before withdrawing a handful of flyers with a triumphant grunt.

As he orders a replacement for the door, I sweep the remaining shards of broken glass.

"You'll need flyers, I guess," I tell him once he's hung up. A glance over my shoulder reveals him to be watching me, slumped against the wall in a position he must find the most comfortable. "That's what Mr. Zhang had made for his reopening."

"I guess I do." He shuffles to another corner of the space and fishes out a sheath of paper and a pen. He flattens the sheet with one hand and starts to sketch. I find myself drifting closer, trying to guess the creature he's forming with stroke after stroke.

Gradually, a woman comes to life. Her large, dark eyes stare from the page, full of questioning wonder. Frizzy bangs. Long, curling hair...

"Very funny," I choke out once his subject becomes painfully obvious.

He doesn't look up, his brow drawn in concentration. Soon, his entire posture shifts, as if he's transcended the pain, too intent on his work. His hand moves steadily, possessed by some unnatural grace that allows him to form delicate lines in one motion and harsher broad strokes the next.

"Rafe?"

He doesn't react, blind to everything but this. Drawing. Creating. Bleeding his thoughts onto paper, shaping reality with the swipe of a pen.

My irritation gives way to shameless awe. Some of the emotion swelling in my chest is pure jealousy.

But the rest?

At some point, I have to mentally separate the woman he's drawing from myself. She's too beautiful. Too mysterious, her gaze so penetrating it's impossible to know what she's thinking. Her expression could convey a million different emotions. Interest. Disinterest. Lust. Wonder. Hate.

She's the type of woman I secretly strive to be. Someone confident. Talented. Prideful.

"Done," Rafe declares, shoving the drawing aside. He reaches into his stash again, this time withdrawing two slips of paper and another pen. "I work. You write," he commands, shoving both toward me.

I bite my lip rather than argue.

He's already starting on another sketch, but I sense his intention is to deliberately provoke me this time. The outline is broader, spanning the width of the entire page. Like magic, a figure forms—someone feminine, slender with bare legs, and a delicately curved torso.

"Nice," I scoff, my cheeks flaming.

He has the nerve to meet my stare without an ounce of humor. "Get to work." He taps my untouched sheet of paper. "A deal's a deal, bunny."

He returns to his task, easily shutting out the world again.

Without taking my eyes from him, I pick up the pen. Hold it to the page. Stall…

Set it aside.

"Write," Rafe demands, dropping all pretense. "Tell me what's in your head, bunny. Right now. Don't hold back. Let me fucking have it."

Asshole, I scribble. But that word bleeds into another, and then an entire sentence. Before I realize it, I'm scribbling down a paragraph, the words disjointed and sloppy, the meaning unclear.

But watching him robs me of the doubt I'm used to fighting.

And I hate him for it.

Envy infects me instead. He's so shameless in his expression. My initial suspicion was right, and a lewd display quickly comes together—a naked woman, lying on her side, her gaze concealing a dare. A taunt. A refusal. A beckoning.

She's an infuriating contradiction, her shape etched with brutal detail. Slender hips, perky breasts, and a proud tilt to her chin. I'm frowning, and my pen drifts, forming a slash across the entire page until I drop the pen altogether.

"Stop!" I slam my hand over his sketch, but the look he gives me. It's utter confusion.

"What?" I don't miss how his hand flutters toward the page as if to shield it from sight before he curls a fist.

"I..." I'm insulted...I think. Why? Because... "That's not me." I wait for him to deny that it was ever supposed to be. "I don't look like that."

Like *that*. Bold, displaying naked, beautiful limbs and a sensual appeal that takes my breath away. My blood boils, heated by another jealous thought—how many of his previous conquests did he mash into that picture?

His frown, however, sends my pulse into overdrive. It isn't guilty, like that of someone caught in a bad joke. Head cocked, he runs his fingers over the creature he's created like a man scouring a map, hunting for where he took a wrong turn.

And it hits me like a punch—I've insulted him. Because, as foreign as this woman is to me, to him...

She *is* me.

"I… I mean." My words falter, stammered, and disjointed. In the end, I wrench my gaze back to my page, grab my pen, and keep writing, shutting off the part of my brain that craves to pour over every word. Every line.

I just spill whatever comes to mind, aware of him watching me.

Eventually, he does the same, adding more detail to his drawing until the glimpses I sneak of it leave me more breathless every time. In a childish way, I could call it magic. How he crafts something from nothing. In a few masterful blends of shadow, he has a window in his hands, displaying the world as he sees it.

And what a cruel, mistrustful, mysterious, watchful, magical world it is.

Sometime during the process, I lose track of writing again and just watch him work.

"You have a gift," I blurt out as he blends his final lines with the pad of his finger. "I mean it, Rafe. You—"

"Do the same shit a kid with a crayon would?" His voice is sufficiently harsh, but his eyes give him away. In them, I catch a hint of the vulnerability he works so hard to shield —rebellious pride for his art.

"Your vision is beautiful," I whisper. "It's so beautiful."

"This is nothing." He flips the page over, but before I can argue, he crooks a finger, beckoning me closer. "Come here."

Curiosity mingles with the thrill inspired by his dangerous grin. Warily, I circle the counter, approaching him with increasing anticipation.

"Turn around." He palms my hips to assist me, and then his fingers find the hem of my shirt. Slowly, he lifts it, exposing the curve of my spine to his touch. I go rigid, paralyzed by the sensation of his breaths warming the hollow between my shoulders before his fingertips land over my skin next. Carefully, he begins to trace a series of invisible designs, and my imagination goes wild.

I don't have to see his face to picture his expression. He'll have his eyes narrowed in concentration, his lower lip seized between his teeth. The same careful way he eyed his canvas.

"You asked me once what I'd tat on you," he murmurs, grazing my spine with the pad of his finger. "I'll show you."

"When?" I'm startled by how eager I sound, but he draws back, letting my shirt fall into place.

"When you let me inside that head of yours. I'll give you whatever you fucking want."

"How?"

I'm left reeling as he pushes past me, lumbering down the back hallway and up the stairs. By the time I manage to follow, he's already returning, fully dressed, wearing a pair of boots, keys in hand.

"Where are you going?" I ask as he shoulders open the door to the alley.

"I'm hungry," he says without looking back. "In the meantime, get to work. I want this place spick and span."

As the door closes behind him, I sense there's more he's left unsaid. Something to do with whatever I glimpsed as he drew, paired with his confession.

He wants to know what's inside my head.

But how, when I barely know the answers myself?

I return to the counter where the two drawings remain. Once again, I'm taken aback at how similar the figure he etched looks to me. At the same time, she's an enigma. I run my fingers over her features before folding the page and tucking it into my pocket.

Eventually, I return to his apartment and find my bag near the couch, my notebook still inside it. Curling up near the window, I press my pen to a fresh page.

Emulating him is harder than it should be. That abandon eludes me, his sheer, focused need to draw an alien concept. I'm left fishing for the right words, unsure of how to start.

He wanted me to show him what it's like inside my head. In essence, it's comparable to being a moth. One drawn to a burning, dazzling flame despite the risks.

It will gladly burn in the aftermath.

And, with that imagery in my head, the floodgates open.

A million different phrases spill out as my mind whirls with images of watchful dark eyes and a body like sin. Soon, the rest of the world fades. My universe narrows to a strip of ink, forming whatever is in my head, but it feels as though I'll never have enough time to get it all out—this confession. These words. This magic.

My only tether to the real world comes in the form of a smell at first—sharp and pungent, savory, and spicy. My stomach growls, shattering the trance, as I look up from the pages of my notebook, I'm so shocked by the sight I find, I drop my pen.

Rafe is in the kitchen, shirt off, back to me as he works at the stove. He's cooking, a realization that catches me off guard almost as much as his voice does—low, forming a jaunty, slightly off-key tune.

By now, the man shouldn't be capable of surprising me—but watching him perform such a domestic task serves that purpose and then some.

"What are you making?" I ask, rising to my feet. My legs throb in protest, and a glance at the sunset painting the horizon beyond the window reinforces just how long I've been writing—I've lost hours in what felt like mere minutes.

"Elotes," Rafe declares as I approach. He presents me with a steaming platter of food balanced on one hand. "And tamales."

"Impressive," I declare, and my awe isn't faked—scrambled eggs and salad is the extent of my culinary abilities.

His creation blows both out of the water. Intrigued, I sample the elote—corn slathered in a mixture of spices—and my eyes widen in genuine shock.

"Good, huh?" Rafe smirks, unabashedly smug. "It's damn good."

Too stunned to argue, I nod and attack my plate in earnest. The variety of spices and rich flavor make me suspect he didn't learn this from a random recipe. "Who taught you to cook?" I ask once I've nearly cleared my plate.

"My mother." His face falls, and guilt hits me like a punch to the stomach.

"I'm sorry," I blurt out, but he shakes his head.

"Don't be. She could make one hell of a tamale." He takes a monstrous bite of his and flashes a grin.

"Tell me about her?"

His eyes darken, growing distant again. In a heartbeat, he's miles away, staring into the past where I can't follow.

Just when I think he's beyond my reach, he sighs.

"She was good," he says softly. "Damn good. A good mother. A good woman. She worked her ass off for me. Anything I wanted, I got, whether or not we could afford it. Even if I didn't deserve it. Somehow, someway, she made it happen."

Obvious sadness deepens his voice, and I have a good idea as to why. Gino once mocked him with the awful truth of just how his mother provided for him—by doing whatever his uncle required of her. Anything for her son.

"I was a punk back then," he adds. "I gave her shit like you wouldn't believe, but she never once yelled at me. Never hit me. Never really punished me. 'You're angry,' she used to say. 'Don't pout or throw a tantrum. You let it out. You show me your pain.' Then she'd give me a pad or a pen and make me draw. No matter how shitty it was, she'd always act like it was a Picasso or some shit."

He laughs, and I feel my lips quirk into a smile.

"She encouraged your art," I say softly.

He frowns as if he never put the pieces together himself. "I guess she did."

"And your dad?" I don't know what makes me broach this topic, but his eyes cut to mine, brimming with an emotion that isn't anywhere near love or affection. It's pain. One so raw, he must normally keep it buried deep. Just as quickly, he smothers it with a hardened mask.

"He was a piece of shit," he says. "She cleaned up at one of Shen's clubs back in the day and was nothing more than a conquest to him."

There's more to it, though. Exhaling, he adds, "He wanted to be a singer or some shit. Break away from the triad. Make something of himself. He fed her so much bullshit about the life he'd build for her, all of it a fantasy. But she never lost faith in that lie, even when he turned his frustration on her."

"He hurt her?"

He strokes his bottom lip, lingering near the bruised flesh. "Yes. He hurt her. Damn near every fucking day during the worst of it. Until he went too far."

He's already told me this part of the story. *One night, he got too rough after showing up again out of the blue. He shoved her around, but she didn't get back up. The asshole just laughed and passed out. She would never call the cops on his ass.*

"You look like her. Your mother," I point out, recalling the picture of the woman I caught a glimpse of in his room. "You have her eyes."

"Her eyes." He scoffs, his upper lip curling from his teeth. I worry I've insulted him, until he brushes his finger along the ridge of his cheekbone as if memorizing the shape. "I have those," he admits, letting his hand fall. "But that's it. Nothing else. I don't even want to be like her."

He sounds too cold. Too bitter.

"Why?" I ask.

"Because she gave it all up for a worthless motherfucker. Everything." He turns away, his hands forming fists. "She sold her soul to a son of a bitch for nothing in return. Nothing but pain and bullshit. What good came of that—"

"She had you." I don't know what makes me say it, but he flinches. Gradually, the fire leaves his eyes, and he's ice in an instant.

"I think she'd be proud of you," I add clumsily. "I know she would."

Slowly… Very slowly, he sets his food aside and approaches me. Each step is deliberate, giving me all the time in the world to evade his reach.

I don't, and his arms go around me, his mouth finding my shoulder. I can feel his heartbeat racing, his breaths heavy and labored. Very gently, his fingers slip into my hair, and the soft, hesitant motions goad me into voicing a confession of my own.

"My mother didn't want me." It sounds so dramatic to say and yet so emotionless at the same time. After twenty-one years, I've made peace with it. The admission doesn't hurt anymore, as natural to utter as my own name. "My dad really wanted a boy, and Branden was her ticket to guaranteed alimony if they divorced. I wasn't part of her plan. I barely even have memories of her, to be honest. She didn't teach me how to cook, and she certainly didn't teach me how to write. She just…existed. Until one day she never came back."

He stiffens, and it strikes me that he may suspect the next part of the story before I even say it.

"She was angry after what happened with Bran. Humiliated. I…" I suck in a breath, self-conscious of the admission on the tip of my tongue. "I envy you. I wish I had your memories. I wish I had something of her to cherish. Something to love—"

"No." Abruptly, he pulls away. "No, you don't."

He heads for the door, and his posture alone warns me from following. His shoulders are tense, his steps stiff.

When he leaves, slamming the door behind him, I don't know what to feel. Something tells me that his anger isn't directed toward me—that doesn't mean I don't feel it.

CHAPTER EIGHT

I wake up with my heart pounding as I struggle to make out my surroundings. Something's wrong. The room itself isn't what has me on edge, but a noise. Persistent, heavy pounding from down below. Scrambling to my feet, I tear through the small layout of Rafe's apartment, alarmed to find that he's still not back.

The only item out of place lies on the coffee table—my journal, still open face down. Even before I lift it, I suspect what page it's on. Sure enough, I'm right—my latest piece.

Reading it over now, I'm struck by how different it reads from my usual writing. There are no pretty, careful lines. No abstract phrases.

In blunt, ugly words, a story forms, plain for anyone to interpret. That of a moth who ventured too close to an enticing flame. Given the horror she was fleeing from, the fire was a fitting end...

A rumble of thunder draws my attention as I set the notebook aside. From the window, I can see the sky, gray with a recent storm, the street still wet below. I don't spot Rafe outside either, but as I start for the stairs, I catch the sound of his voice.

"Ah, fuck!"

Downstairs, I find him crouched before the entrance of the shop, wrestling a new door into place. He spots me from over his shoulder and jerks his chin. "Give me a hand, would ya? Hold it here."

I step closer, grabbing the glass frame where he indicates. As he fiddles with a set of metal hinges and screws, I scan his face, hunting for any hint of emotion. Paranoia whispers cruel insinuations of where he could have been.

With Bonnie?

Someone else?

His hair gives me a clue—mussed, slightly damp, matching the soaked pavement outside that betrays overnight rain. He's wearing the same jeans from yesterday too, his chest bare, the dragon on full display.

"Hey!" He nearly drops a screw and shoots me a stern look. "Focus, bunny. I spent too much money on this piece of shit to break it now."

I comply, assisting until he finally has the support in place, and the door stands on its own.

"Good, now go change," he tells me. "You're on the clock, bunny. I spoke to Zhang. Starting today, you work for me, and I won't tolerate your bullshit."

He swaggers into the back room, but I sense from the distance he puts between us that he's still stuck on whatever upset him last night. I toy with the idea of prodding him to tell me what. Instead, I go upstairs, shower, and change into fresh clothing—all my own this time.

Rafe doesn't say a word when I return to find him in the shop's front, arranging materials over the counter. When he finally looks up, his eyes graze over my modest sweater without a reaction.

"Sort these," he commands, shoving a stack of documents my way. "Disclaimers and shit. Anyone who wants a tat needs to sign one, got it?"

He's already gone before I can reply, arranging his supplies and tools on a table across the room. Warily, I creep behind the counter and organize the paperwork. All the while, that awkward tension between us grows, seeping into every interaction. Him handing me a handful of pens feels equivalent to a challenger arming an opponent in a silent war.

He moves stiffly with more than just the pain from his injuries. Any step that takes him away from me is quick, but any that brings him closer carries a speed reminiscent of someone wading through quicksand.

It surprisingly isn't long before the door opens, introducing new people into our dynamic—customers. They look to be tourists, going off their oversized shirts and casual attire. They wander the shop aimlessly as Rafe points out various hanging designs and names prices.

I quickly lose track of my supposed task by watching him. In this instance, he sports a different mask from his cocky swagger or ice-cold aloofness. He's approachable and informative but stern, conveying knowledge of both tattoos and his capabilities to apply one in a way I don't expect. With a few words, he's able to soothe a jittery twenty-something who consents to have a design applied to her ankle.

"I need the paperwork," Rafe snaps to me.

When everything is signed, Rafe guides the client to a leather chair in the center of the room and gets to work.

He's slow and methodical, utilizing the necessary tools with the same care he does his pens. He cleans the area, marks out a rough outline before implanting the actual tattoo using a mechanical object eerily similar to that of a gun.

Roughly an hour later, the client is beaming at his creation, and he has one happy customer down. More are already in the process of following, streaming in and out of the shop to eye the artwork or for consultations.

His flyers must have done the trick. It feels like barely a few minutes go by before someone new enters. As the latest visitor leaves, Rafe cuts his gaze to me.

"What's wrong?" I ask, alarmed by his expression.

"Get out," he hisses. "Now."

"W-What?" I follow his gaze to the front door and spot the beautiful woman about to enter. I barely manage to scramble into the back hallway before the bell above the door chimes.

"Hey Chan," Rafe says. "How you holding up?"

I crane my neck as far as I dare and spot Mara near the front display, her eyes downcast and devoid of makeup. Even her outfit is relatively modest—a T-shirt and jeans.

"I can't believe she's gone," she murmurs, and guilt hits me like a slap to the face. Faith. I've been so worried for myself, I never stopped to think about what Mara might be going through. "I mean, I didn't know her that well," she adds as Rafe draws up beside her. "But it's just so awful. Everyone's shaken up about it."

"It sucks," Rafe agrees. "But don't beat yourself up about it. She wouldn't want you to."

"I know." She sheepishly meets his gaze. "Can I ask you for a favor, though? There's a memorial service planned for tomorrow night—I think your uncle is helping to host it."

Rafe crosses his arms. Is he surprised by that revelation?

"Well, her family wanted a private burial," Mara adds. "But they're allowing this one for anyone who might want to pay their respects. Could you go with me?"

Rafe runs a hand along his jaw, his hesitation apparent.

"My parents are going, but they'll be keeping the Wens company all night, and I don't think I can stomach that. I know it's pathetic, but I at least want to stop by. I would have asked my friend to come with me, but I can't get a hold of her. Please?"

"Alright," Rafe agrees. "I'll go."

Mara beams. "Thank you. I'll even buy you dinner after if you want. I truly appreciate it." She brushes her hand along his shoulder, but he backs away.

"Yeah, no problem." He adjusts the paperwork on the counter, extending the distance between them. "Don't mention it."

"You're probably really busy," Mara says with a nervous laugh. "I nearly passed out when I saw the flyers that you were opening up your client list. I think I can name at least ten people right off the bat who would love to sport a design by you. Myself included." Her cheeks flush prettily, her dark eyes gleaming. "Please tell me that you aren't already booked out for all of eternity?"

Rafe inclines his head for her to approach him. "I think I can make an exception. Here—" he snatches a portfolio from the counter and offers it to her.

Mara flips through the pages, and I figure my expressions must mirror hers every time I view his art. Wide-eyed. Mystified. Seconds from drooling. Admittedly, she seems more impressed by the figure who owns the book than by anything inside it.

"You are so good," she gushes, eyeing him through her lashes. "Do you do tattoos all over?"

"Where are you thinking?" Rafe questions, his gaze on whatever design she's eyeing now.

"Hmm… What about here?" She places the book on the counter and lifts her shirt to expose her sternum and the very edge of a lacy black bra. "I heard some guys find this location sexy."

I hate the jealousy that ignites in my chest, catching my cheeks on fire. A fire fed by the way Rafe's eyes skim the flesh in question.

"Ah… Those hurt like a motherfucker," he warns after clearing his throat.

Mara shrugs. "I trust you," she says. "You'd be gentle with me, right?"

"Right," Rafe says, shifting to a different area of the counter. "So, you wanna schedule? I can fit you in next week."

"So far away?" She pouts, somehow managing to look beautiful and playful at the same time.

They hash out the details until her leaving is finally signaled by the chime of the doorbell. The second I creep from the hall, Rafe sighs.

"Don't fucking look at me like that," he snaps.

"Like what?"

"Like…" He rakes a hand through his hair in frustration. "Like I just fucked her over the counter. And maybe I *should* have. As often as she's been sniffing around my ass, she definitely seems to want it."

"I didn't say anything," I point out—but I don't deny the jealousy either.

"You didn't have to." He storms to the front door and switches the sign from open to closed, locking it from the inside. "I can see it all over your fucking face. And why shouldn't I be attracted to her, huh? You know how many assholes would go for that? I told you once, bunny. I don't do relationships."

But his posture alone warns me that his mood has nothing to do with Mara. He's breathing too quickly, his shoulders tense, hands in fists.

"What's wrong?" I demand, cutting to the chase.

"Wrong?" He barks out a harsh laugh. "Maybe it's time I got some new pussy?"

It takes everything I have in me not to take the bait. He's goading me on purpose, trying to get me to snap, much like a bullfighter waving red.

"You've been like this all morning." I come close enough to place my hand on his back, but he jerks away. "Tell me what's wrong."

"What you wrote… Was it true?"

I stiffen at the heat in his tone. Anger? Judgment?

Was it true—everything I can remember spilled out onto a page.

"Was it?" he demands.

"Yes."

He whirls around and grabs my waist, lifting me off my feet. Two steps back bring us to the counter, and he sets me on top of it, stepping in between my legs.

"Where do you see this going, huh?" he demands, palming the contours of my body through my sweater. "After... Or is this just a fling? A game. You flout mommy and daddy's wishes for a few days and then go crawling back. To them. To him. To the rules, and the money and the boring fucking life you hate. What is this?" He gestures around us with a wave of his hand. "Rebellion? How soon before you go running back to Bran, brother, or not? Just fucking tell me so at least I'm not surprised."

"I can't go back." Hearing it out loud makes my chest tighten, and my eyes burn with the threat of tears. Hope? And terror. I've been lying to myself for so long. Admitting the truth feels comparable to ripping away a Band-Aid and reopening the wound underneath.

"I can't," I repeat. "If I wanted to, I'd be gone by now."

He frowns, still suspicious. I have no choice but to broach the one topic I've successfully avoided until now.

I tell him about Branden's ultimatum, and his expression transforms from rage to disgust.

"That's fucked up," he snarls. "That's—"

"I'm still here." I loop my arms around his neck, trusting him to support my weight. He does, sliding his palms beneath my butt as his heavy sigh rustles my hair.

"Damn," he says. "Do you really think he'd go through with it?"

I shrug. "He wants to control me. He'll do whatever he thinks he has to in order to do that."

He grabs one of my hands from his shoulder, interlacing our fingers. "I've got you," he says softly. "Whether it's for a day. A week. However long you need me, I've got you."

I'm not brave enough to ask him just what that entails. *Me*, with a side of Mara, or Bonnie, or whoever else on the side?

Speaking of Mara…

"I can't keep hiding here forever," I confess tiredly. "Sooner or later, Mr. Zhang… Mara. They're going to find out where I am anyway. How do you feel about that?"

"How?" He raises an eyebrow. "A sexy motherfucker with a sexy bunny at his pad? Trust me, I'll get over the embarrassment."

But he doesn't go further than that, refusing to define our relationship between any definitive boundaries. The sad part? It's not like I even have the right to question that.

So, I take the easy way out by changing the subject. "Do people really get tattoos here?"

I copy Mara by lifting my sweater, but his reaction is the difference between night and day. He strokes his chin, eyeing the bared flesh with renewed interest.

"Here?" He runs his finger down the center of my ribcage, rousing a million goosebumps. "I wasn't lying when I said it hurts like a bitch." But he continues tracing the flesh there, mapping out an invisible design.

I lift my sweater entirely, setting it aside.

Any unease I might feel dies the instant I meet his gaze. I have his full attention, and I lean back, exposing his "canvas" to use as he sees fit.

"Show me?"

A wicked smile shapes his mouth as he crosses the room for a pen. When he returns, however, his focus shifts. Even as he palms my breast, I sense that he's one-hundred-percent intent on the task at hand.

He's an artist at work.

Observing him hunched over paper is one thing, but this... It's an experience in itself. He manipulates the pen expertly, and the design comes to life, stunning in every sense of the word.

"Rafe..."

"Don't speak," he scolds while applying a bit of shading with meticulous care. "Just stay like this. Just like this."

The more he works, the easier that command becomes to uphold—I'm too awestruck to do anything but stare.

Even from this angle, the image spreading across my ribcage is beyond anything I could have expected. Not a bunny. Not even a dragon...

"You read what I wrote."

He's already admitted as much. It's still surreal to see it unfolding—that of the moth and her flame.

"I wrote about you," I whisper, bringing my fingers to his jaw. They're shaking—he feels hot enough to burn, tensing beneath my touch. "And you got what you wanted, right? A look inside my head."

He doesn't bother to say as much out loud. He just draws, utilizing every ounce of flesh at his discretion to bring to life the creature I'd centered my writing around.

A moth, its wings beautifully singed, its detail exquisite. But the feature that makes my throat tighten is something I didn't mention in my scrawled tale. He drew a large, watchful eye on either side of the insect's body, staring impassively at the world, guarding their secrets.

I don't know how much time passes before he finally sets the pen aside and stands, running his hands through his hair. "What do you think—"

I arch toward him, my lips finding his, silencing his startled grunt. Closing my eyes, I relax into the feel of this moment, blinding myself to everything else.

In so many ways, the mock-tattoo feels like the perfect expression of *everything*. Every obscure emotion and inane concept I'd never be able to put into words.

But it's also a warning—what awaits me at the end of this, whatever this is.

Broken wings and searing flame.

CHAPTER NINE

I wake up in Rafe's bed, but this time I'm not alone. He lies next to me, his hand thrown over my waist, his scent in my lungs. I can't resist stroking my fingers through his hair, marveling at the sight of him like this, vulnerable for once, his body devoid of tension.

Some of his injuries look slightly better in the pale dawn light, including the one on his chest. I inch closer, tentatively brushing my fingers over the ridge of his pec.

"Damn, bunny." He opens his eyes, focusing on me. "I thought waking up with your head near my dick was torture enough. You had to go and kick it up a notch."

His words trigger an impulse only he has ever inspired in me. I rise onto my hands and knees, inching back toward the end of the mattress, aware that I have his full attention.

His confusion quickly morphs into shock as I slip my hand between his legs, urging them to part. He does slowly, creating a large enough space for me to crawl in between them while lacing my fingers around the waistband of his sweatpants.

As I drag them down partway, my chest heaves, revealing the trail of dark curls shielding what lies below. I look up to find him watching me avidly, his upper body propped on his elbows.

"Keep going," he commands hoarsely.

I do, easing the fabric down as he shifts to assist me. I'm soon faced with a part of him I've felt in the most intimate way possible. He's beautiful—reddening flesh mapped by a crisscrossing of swollen veins. Carefully, I reach out, tracing the path of one.

I've barely gone an inch as he grits his teeth, his head rearing back against his shoulders. "Fuck, I need you to—"

He can't even put it into words. Instead, he lunges for my wrist and directs my hand downward, and it's as if I can read *his* mind for once.

Open your hands. Like that.

Grip me harder. Harder.

"Shit, bunny." He fists his free hand over the sheets. Soon, a request becomes apparent, written across his gaze as if in blazing neon letters.

Slowly, I sink to my belly with my legs dangling off the end of the bed. Any doubt vanishes the second I see his face. His wet lips slightly parted, his gaze so intent on me that I almost fear I'll combust from the force of it, honed like the full intensity of the sun.

It's cruel how long I make him wait, hovering with my mouth dangerously close to where he craves it the most. Needs it. A vein in his neck jumps the second I brush my tongue along the tip of him, and I'm startled by the taste. Musky. Powerful. Not offensive.

"Jesus," he groans, watching like a hawk as I take him in as deeply as I dare.

A list of supposed actions—all overheard from Mara in vivid detail—cross my mind, only to fade beneath a wave of pleasure that shocks me to my core. Electrifies. Emboldens me.

I stop thinking and focus on wringing every gasp and grunt from him that I can.

"Stop!" He cradles my scalp in his hands, urging me off of him.

My confused glance is met with a growl as he flips me over, straddling my hips. He makes short work of my skirt and shirt. Then, our lips meet, his easily overpowering mine as his hand slips between my legs, easing a finger inside me.

My readiness makes him groan as he rocks his hips to replace the digit with a larger appendage. He thrusts in hard, letting my body greedily adjust to his size.

It's a sinful cross between pleasurable and painful. Then he strokes out, and in again, and it's fire. My mind reels with how vital an act can seem, though you've gone most of your life without it. How a single touch, kiss, and bit of contact can rival any other desire life has to offer. It's like my body didn't know what *feeling* truly was until it learned to grapple with the invasion of his.

The sheer depth of what it can be like to be known by someone else so deeply.

How dangerous it can feel to burn beneath another's body heat.

How good.

How reckless.

How destructive.

IT'S ONLY in the early afternoon when Rafe finally drags himself from the mattress long enough to heat up some food. We devour leftover tamales at the counter, and he eyes the time on the microwave with a curse.

"I've got some shit I've gotta take care of," he says, setting his plate aside. His eyes cut toward the door, and I wonder if the 'shit' on his mind has anything to do with the ultimate destination of the briefcase we took from the warehouse.

"And Faith's service is tonight. I should really go see Mara," I add, forced to face the reality of just how terrible a friend I've been to her.

"And what are you going to tell her?" Rafe wonders. His back is to me, obscuring his reaction. From his tone alone, I can't tell just what he wants to hear. For me to keep our fling secret? Or save him the hassle of having to avoid Mara's attempts at flirtation.

"I don't know."

"Do you want me to drive you?" he asks. "In case you run into him?"

I suck in a breath and try to imagine what could be worse. Facing Branden alone, or pitting him against Rafe? I quickly decide on an answer and shake my head. "I'll be fine."

"Fine," he repeats before turning on his heel and padding down the hall as I gape in alarm.

"Rafe?" I start to follow, but he's already returning, an item in hand.

"Take this." He hands me a small device that takes my brain a second to identify—a cell phone, a much more modern style than my old one.

Gratitude is a living thing, threatening to crawl up my throat. "Thank you."

"My number's in it," he adds, starting for the stairs. He's already thrown on a fresh pair of clothing and donned his boots. Clenched in one of his hands is the handle of that infamous case. "I'll see you tonight."

He looks back as if to gauge how I'll respond to the invitation.

"Okay," I say with a nod. "Tonight."

He heads down the stairs, taking them two at a time. From the base of them, he calls back, "And take the spare key. It's on the hook."

Sure enough, I spy one, hanging from the same spot he kept his car keys.

I take my time showering and getting dressed before arranging my hair in the best way possible to cover most of the bruising. In the end, I leave it down and sigh in defeat. To be honest, the worst of the bruising is already starting to fade, leaving brownish splotches around my eye and down my chin.

Ironically, my neck looks the most ravaged, sporting fresher, bright red spots from this morning. When I finally leave the shop, I take the back roads to the restaurant district, jumping at any sudden noise to pierce the quiet.

I'm not ready for the true depths of paranoia that descend the further I go. Every person passing by morphs and transforms into someone else. Branden. Then I blink, and they reform into a businessman, a passing child, or another stranger. And each time, it's like I can hear him, scoffing at my attempts at normalcy.

You're a video star now, Hannah. You're a fucking slut. A liar. A whore. Say cheese…

"Hannah!" I blink and nearly run into the smiling figure who races forward to greet me. "I've been looking all over for you, girl!" Mara explains, throwing her arms around my shoulders. "It's like you fell off the face of the earth. Where the hell have you been?" She draws back, and her expression transforms as her mouth drops open, her eyes widening. "Oh my god. What happened to your face?"

She runs her finger across my cheek, but I gently evade her touch and force what I hope passes for a smile. "Would you believe that I ran into a door? I'm so clumsy."

"You ran into a door," she says, deadpanned. Her raised eyebrow betrays her true thoughts on that explanation, but I race to change the subject before she can say as much out loud.

"I heard about Faith. I'm so sorry."

"Yeah." She frowns, real sadness shaping her features. "It feels kind of weird to be pushing noodles, all things considered."

This time of day, foot traffic is light, the lunch rush over. Judging from her outfit—a black blouse and skirt—she must have been manning the hostess station of her parents' restaurant and saw me approach.

"So, where the hell have you been, Dewitt?" she demands, placing her hands on her hips. "I've tried calling you. Don't tell me your charger is still 'lost.'"

"Try my phone, actually," I say. It isn't a complete lie. To prove it, I withdraw the one Rafe gave me. "I have a new one."

"Nice," Mara says with genuine admiration. She snatches it and programs her number in before handing it back. "I wanted one of those, but they're fucking expensive. Anyway, where have you been?"

"I decided to go with my brother to the beach for a few days." God, it's almost terrifying how easily the lies come. *Because it's all you're good at, Hannah*, a part of me hisses. *Just like Branden says. You're a liar.*

"Oh, well… Now that you're back, we should totally hang out. I know it's kind of morbid, but Faith's memorial service is tonight—not like a funeral or anything. You don't have to dress up. Rafe said he'd go with me, but—"

"I'll go with you."

She smiles. "Thank God. At least I'll have a wingman for if I fall flat on my face again. Like damn, I know it's utterly trashy to try to pick up a guy at a memorial, but I just don't get this one. I mean, from what I hear, he's fucked half the girls in this town. But *I* practically flash my titties at him and…" She trails off, blushing. "Never mind. But damn, it's like some kind of personal conquest now. I will fuck that asshole or die trying. It's the principle of the matter."

"You're too good for him, Mara," I blurt out. "Besides, you could have any guy you want."

"But I want that guy," she declares, stubbornly jutting her chin. Her teeth seize her lower lip as she groans. "And he is so sexy. And nice—I heard from my parents that he offered to pay for Faith's funeral expenses as well as the reward for any information on her case. Five thousand dollars."

"He did?" I don't know why the thought surprises me.

Maybe because it brings one good point into question—what was the nature of his relationship with Faith in the first place?

"He did," Mara insists with a nod. "Let me tell my folks I'm on break, and then we can catch up on all of the gossip. You've missed a lot, girl. And I want to hear all about this 'vacation' that left you with even more hickies on your neck than before."

I feel my cheeks catch fire as I brush my hand along my throat. Even with the high neckline of my sweater, the marks are obvious.

"I hope the same culprit isn't responsible for the 'door' you ran into," she adds pointedly. "I know you don't have a lot of experience with guys, Han, but trust me. Anyone who puts their hands on you isn't worth the dick."

"It's not like that," I say, brushing my hair forward to cover most of the bruising. "But I will take you up on that lunch offer."

"Great!" She skips off, entering the Chans' restaurant, and I instinctively start to follow her as the back of my neck heats with awareness.

A glance over my shoulder reveals no one in sight—but I feel it. He's here, watching me…

"You ready?" Mara asks, appearing by my side, a black leather purse in hand. "Let's go. I'm starving."

I follow her, but the uneasy dread in my gut only intensifies, lasting through our entire walk to a nearby café.

And I swear that this time, the figure I catch as I glance behind me isn't a figment of my imagination.

CHAPTER TEN

"So, who are you fucking, and for how long?" Mara questions from over the rim of her latte. Winking, she smacks her glossy lips together and leans over her pink place setting. "Tell me everything."

We're seated at a table near the front windows, which provide a good view of the main street—and anyone who might happen to walk by. I can't stop my gaze from darting to it every few seconds just to scan the foot traffic. So far, I've only noticed a few workers dressed in business attire or the average tourist. No Branden. Yet.

"Hey!" Mara reaches over the table to tap my shoulder, and I reluctantly turn my attention back to her. "Spill, bitch," she demands. "I've told you about all the assholes I've fucked. Your turn."

"He's…" I swallow hard as the truth sticks to the back of my throat. Coming clean now would be the smart thing to do. The right thing. For whatever reason, I can't make myself form the words. "No one."

Mara raises an eyebrow. "No one. Damn, I didn't know the 'air' was into rough sex. I guess I've been masturbating all wrong—"

"Mara!" I steal a sip from my coffee if only to disguise how my cheeks flame. "You are so bold." Forcing a laugh, I fake a smile that she doesn't return.

"Fine," she snaps, rolling her eyes. "We'll leave that topic— for now. So how is the writing going? You get your essay done yet?"

"Not yet."

"The deadline's coming up," she warns. "Not that I'm one to talk. It feels like I haven't written anything good in ages. Like my sexual frustration is translating to a creative block. Damn Rafe Wei-Shen!"

"You said he's slept with everyone?" I ask only to instantly regret doing so. It's a dangerous topic to broach.

Dangerous, and at the same time, too tempting to ignore.

Mara nods. "Almost everyone. The sexy people, anyway. One could say he has a type—big tits and a bigger ass. But he's strictly transactional. His conquests give him what he wants, and he'll give them a shopping spree or two. Maybe some cash. I hear he's even into threesomes." She giggles. "Hey, maybe if I text him to come over with *you* here, he might bite?"

"Don't," I croak as she brandishes her phone for emphasis.

Still giggling, she stows it beneath the table, though I can't see if she's typing a text from here.

Her eyes meet mine, suddenly stern. "Though... On a serious note, rumor has it, he was seeing Faith before she died. Bad boys, I can do. Murderers? No go."

"What?" It's like the universe narrows to this table, and everything else disappears. I'm biting my lip, so hard I taste copper though I don't feel anything.

"Yeah," Mara says, sounding miles away. "Someone I know said he saw them together a lot at his club. And he helped in the search for her, and now that he's paying for her funeral, well it makes sense. But baby boy isn't the sentimental type. He must have really liked her. Or," she adds, lowering her voice conspiratorially. "He feels guilty. It's not public knowledge, but I heard from my parents—who have been trying to keep the Wens company with everything going on—that Faith's phone is missing. Maybe someone didn't want it found? Like, she could have had tons of nudes on it or something, though Rafe doesn't strike me as the type to be embarrassed by that. Hey... Are you okay?" She snaps her fingers beneath my nose until she has my full attention. "You went all space cadet there for a minute."

"I'm fine," I insist, but I'm already scanning the window again, this time in search of a distraction. Anything to get my mind off the selfish, sordid thoughts circling my brain.

But as a familiar figure comes into view, I realize that I got my wish.

"Good," Mara says, oblivious to how I stiffen in my seat. "Because I need you to help me plan the sexiest outfit ever that one could realistically wear to a memorial service—"

"Oh, no." The exclamation slips out the second I realize that the specter crossing the street doesn't disappear when I blink. *Liam*, heading straight for the café's entrance. He must be off, sporting a plain white shirt and jeans instead of his uniform, but he looks anything but relaxed.

He's angry.

"Hannah?" Mara exclaims as I lurch to my feet. I don't even think I choke out an explanation to her as I scramble for the exit.

I'm so focused on making it outside that I nearly run into someone on my way out of the door. He grabs my arm before I can pull away. One look at his face and I can tell he isn't here by accident.

"Hannah?" Narrowed and focused, his eyes latch onto me with an intensity I've never seen from him.

"Liam…" I croak. Self-consciously, I lift my hand to shield the worst of the bruising, but it's too late.

Without invitation, he brushes his thumb along my cheek, gingerly prodding the skin. Concern unfurls across his face, hardening the already stern tilt to his mouth. He doesn't look surprised. Just resigned. "Damn, Hannah. What happened? Branden said you were okay, but—"

"What did he tell you?" I demand, unable to keep the alarm from my voice. I whip around, hunting for any hint of my brother lurking nearby.

The street is nearly empty, and when I return to Liam, he looks taken aback. "He didn't say much," he admits. "Just that you were in some kind of trouble."

I suck in a breath to disguise my unease. Just how many lies is Branden spinning about me?

"I tried to check on you at the bookstore," Liam adds. "Luckily, I happened to see you walk this way. Are you okay?"

"I'm fine." I try to pull away, but he's persistent, trailing his thumb beneath my injured eye.

"That's not what I'm worried about," he admits. "I'm not an idiot, Hannah. These days you look like you're haunted. I've been worried about you. If you tell me what's wrong, I can—"

"I'm fine," I insist more forcefully this time. "I promise. Thank you for worrying, but you don't have to. But... Maybe you can help me with something else."

Rafe's suspicions keep bouncing around in my head. Now seems like as good a time as any to get some answers.

"What?" Liam asks.

For a second, I toy with the idea of how to spin the question as sneakily as possible. How to lie. Deceive. In the end, I come to the honest truth—there is no other way to put it than bluntly. "What do you know about the Wen murder case?"

His brow furrows as his thumb stills near the corner of my mouth. "Not much," he admits. "It's considered high profile due to all the exposure. Most of what I know is just gossip."

But his eyes flicker away from mine, suddenly evasive.

"I heard there might be other girls who have gone missing," I say, trying a different tack. "And Faith worked at this club. I think it's called Stella's. Do the police know anything about—"

"Stella's?" His tone is a fraction harder. Definitely more suspicious than shocked. Slowly, he withdraws his hand from my face, letting it fall to his side. "Hannah, what is this about?"

"One of my friends knew Faith," I say, which isn't technically a lie, and I allow my real desperation to leech into my voice, strengthening the claim. "I want to give her whatever comfort I can regarding the investigation. Is there anything at all you can tell me? Even something small. Please."

He sighs and shoots a glance over his shoulder before leaning in toward me.

"Well…I know they have one suspect," he admits. "I don't know who exactly. Just that he sent the last known message to her phone."

I feel my eyes widen as I recall what the officer told Rafe the other day. "I thought they couldn't find her phone?"

"They're keeping it hush for now," he says, stiffening as a group of people walk by, none of whom seem interested in our conversation. Stepping closer to me, he adds, "Her phone was wiped. They were able to pull some of her texts via her cloud, but not everything. Some of it was encrypted, I think. They also questioned one of her friends. A Lylah, something, about some guy who might have been giving her trouble."

It takes everything I have to keep any ounce of recognition from my face. Lylah. Was she the same girl Rafe and I talked to? If so, the police could know all about the mysterious DW. "What did she say?"

Liam shakes his head. "Look, I shouldn't even be telling you this stuff. Now you tell *me* something. What happened to you?"

I force another quick smile and pivot on my heel toward the café. "It's nothing. I should really get going—"

"Then let me ask you about something else," Liam says. "I googled her. That girl you told me about. Lexi Winacott."

My feet stop listening to my brain, and I nearly trip before stopping short entirely. "You what?"

I sense his steps approach before his hand settles over my shoulder. "I'm so sorry you had to go through that, Hannah. I'm so sorry. If you need to talk about it, I'm here. I mean that. About you. About Branden... About anything. I'm not saying this out of duty, either. I care about you—"

"Branden," I rasp, whirling around to face him. "Did you tell him? About Lexi? Did you?"

He tilts his jaw, his eyes unreadable. "No. Should I?" He scans my face as if hunting for a certain reaction. Whatever he finds makes him ask in a softer tone, "Has he told you what's been going on with him lately? I know it's none of my business, but..."

"What do you mean?" Dread builds in my stomach, impossible to hide any longer. Licking my lips, I once again aim for the truth. "About his suspension?"

From the way he purses his lips, he looks almost...relieved. "He told you then," he says with a sharp nod. "He made me swear not to say anything, but I've been worried about him lately—what's wrong?"

I can only imagine how I must look.

Horrified?

Behind Liam, a living shadow darts from across the street, heading straight for us. My brain identifies him instantly, but I'm nowhere near fast enough to head him off.

"Rafe!" I shout uselessly. "Don't!"

It's too late.

Too enraged, he doesn't seem to hear me. In a blur of motion, he rams into Liam from behind, nearly taking him off his feet with one blow. His fist already poised for another, his upper lip drawn from his teeth in a mask of sheer rage.

I stagger between them, trying to brace my hand against Rafe's chest. Solid muscle ripples beneath my palm, impossible to control. It's like trying to stop a charging bull. With little effort, he pushes past me, singularly focused on his target.

"Don't," I shout, clawing at his forearm. "Rafe, don't! It's not him! He's not Bran!"

He draws back suddenly, his fist still raised, eyes blazing without a shred of confusion contributing to the anger. Just rage. Fury. Betrayal. The second they fixate on me, I realize the truth. He *knows*. Whether he figured out before he hit Liam, or after, doesn't matter, he knows now.

And his rage hits me like a blowtorch, scorching whatever pathetic excuses I had prepared for this moment.

All I can do is reach for him, sick with guilt. "I'm sorry. I'm so sorry—"

"Fuck you." He squares his shoulders, turning on his heel despite the commotion swirling to life in his wake. Alarmed bystanders gape as Liam swipes at his nose. It's bleeding.

"Let me help." I rush to him and fish through my purse for a spare napkin. "Here."

"What the hell was that about?" he demands, staring after Rafe, who's already halfway down the block. "Do you know that guy?"

I say nothing, and when the worst of the bleeding stops, Liam shrugs me off. "I've gotta get to work," he says, swiping at his nose. With his free hand, he snatches something from his pocket and presses it into my hand. "Here. If you need me, I'm on tonight. Damn it, that asshole's lucky I don't press charges."

"Don't," I plead, but he's already crossing the street, still clutching at his nose.

It isn't until I finally turn to face the café that another realization hits with the strength of a gut punch. *Mara.* I race back to our table only to find her already gone. The check has been paid but scrawled across the bottom of the receipt is a simple message—*Thanks for being such a good friend.*

Feeling slapped, I leave the café and start down the block, hunting for any sign of her. What I'll say if I do find her, I have no idea.

But she's gone. I don't even find her near the Chans' restaurant. Desperate, I try texting her, but minutes pass without a response.

I keep walking as I wait for one, melding with the afternoon foot traffic. I'm halfway across town before I realize—I have nowhere to go.

Rafe's feels off-limits, and my old lease runs out in just a few short days. My only haven is a building I find myself approaching out of habit.

I nearly sigh in relief once I find the Paper Crane is open, blazing with light as the sun starts to set. A few customers litter the shop as I enter and see Mr. Zhang at the counter. He eyes me warily, lingering over my bruises.

"I heard you were taking off for a few days," he says without broaching any other topic.

"Yeah, well… I'm back," I say, unable to come up with any reasonable excuse. The pity in his gaze warns that I don't have to, and I feel bold enough to ask for the one thing I don't have a right to. A distraction. "If you want me to close up, I can."

"Hmm." He eyes me for what feels like a solid minute. Then he nods and grabs his bowler hat from a hook on the wall. "I'll head home early. You can close out the register too. And there's an envelope," he adds, his voice low with double meaning.

Too grateful to argue, I watch him go, mulling over what Rafe revealed about him. Could such a kind, hardworking man have a darker vice?

Though, who is anyone really beyond the façade they present to the world? To so many, Branden is the perfect gentleman, an upstanding citizen. The paragon of goodness and an inspiration to people like Liam.

But inside? Darkness dwells within him, too entrenched to overcome.

Speaking of Liam...

I'd shoved whatever he'd given me into my pocket. Unfurling it now, I realize it's a business card, complete with his number. Despite the chaos that unfolded today, my brain keeps coming back to one image again and again. The way he looked at me when I mentioned Branden's suspension.

That strange, unexpected reaction flickered across his face too quickly to appreciate in full then. Pouring over it now, I'm confident enough to name it for what it was.

Hope. Like he wanted to say more but wasn't sure how.

My brother is good at maintaining his façade, but what if even Liam has seen through it?

A conflicting array of emotions wash over me, setting my skin on fire and making my hands shake. The doubt is the worst part, the uncertainty.

For a dangerous second, I play with the prospect of telling Liam everything.

But even trying to imagine Branden's retaliation makes me shrink from the thought. As I settle behind the counter, my mind turns to another topic I've been deliberately avoiding —the video. Would he really upload it? Has he done it already?

I scan the various patrons perusing the bookshelves. Will one of them happen to stumble across a video of a girl having sex in her bed with a man adorned by a dragon tattoo?

The act itself isn't what makes me feel so helpless; I have to blink back tears. It's what it conveys. The lack of control over my own body cuts deep, more violating than any other action Branden's taken so far.

Except, maybe in the old days. In those memories, I've spent years avoiding. They feel as foreign to me now as old, dusty photographs tucked into a box at the back of a basement or attic.

The days of Lexi, and Branden, and the twisted ending to that saga.

"Excuse me?"

I startle to awareness and find a woman standing before me, holding a book.

"I'd like to buy this, please," she says.

"Sure." I ring her up and turn my attention to the remaining customers. By the time closing approaches, I've seen a steady stream of business, more than enough to distract from my thoughts. When the store is finally empty, I take my time cleaning up before stepping out into the night.

Now what? A part of me wonders.

A glance at my phone reveals an absence of text messages from either Rafe or Mara. All I can do is stare at the clock, pouring over my options. Should I go back to my old apartment? Wait for Branden to track me down, if he isn't on my heels already?

Or go to Rafe...

He's probably with Mara now, heading to Faith's memorial. I don't have a right to feel a damn thing about it, especially not jealousy.

Not that he'd need a reason to move on, that hateful voice in my head taunts. *He told you before—you're just a fling—a diversion.*

Even so, they both deserve an apology in person.

I exit the bookstore and find myself heading toward the park Mara mentioned. The service itself isn't hard to spot— a circle of ethereal orange, the result of the assembled crowd, and each attendee holding a lit candle. As I approach, a woman hands me my own as well as a brochure sporting a smiling photo of Faith. I flinch at the image. She looks so happy. So innocent.

Could Branden really be responsible for her death?

I squash the thought without deciding on an answer and creep closer to the circle of mourners. It's too dark to make out anyone from this distance. I have to wander from person to person as a speaker recites a list of Faith's attributes.

I listen avidly, caught off guard by the depth of emotions each speaker conveys. It's a beautiful if somber service. But I don't see Mara or Rafe. It isn't until my third trip around the gathering that I spot two figures who make my heart sink with recognition. The first thing I notice is a pathetic, selfish observation—they resemble a couple. The man is taller, his arm protectively thrown around the woman's shoulders. It isn't until they pass the glow cast by a lit candle that my suspicions are confirmed.

Rafe spots me first, his gaze rigid and indecipherable. Without taking his eyes off me, he murmurs something to Mara and pulls away. Deliberately, he takes a step in another direction, but a sharp jerk of his head warns me to follow.

My heart pounds with every step I take, letting him lead me away from the gathering to a quieter section of the park. The second I'm close enough to touch him, I rush to speak. "I'm sorry—"

"Save it," he snaps. In the dark, his features take on an angular, fearsome appearance. In a way, he seems more like his dragon than human. "I don't want to hear your fucking excuses. I'm done. You want to fuck your 'brother,' then, who am I to stop you?" A harsh laugh punctuates the taunt, making my cheeks flame.

"I wasn't lying about Bran," I say in a rush. "But… The man you've seen me with isn't him. His name is Liam. He's just a friend."

He rolls his eyes, hissing in annoyance. "Where have I heard that line before? A friend. Like Mara is your 'friend,' right? The one you've let try to fuck me left and right? Well, maybe it's time I finally did."

In a blur of motion, he surges past me in the direction of the ongoing service.

Eyeing his retreating back, I've never felt so damn pathetic. "I'm sorry," I say.

He stops mid-step, but if I were to hope I've convinced him, the glare he aims over his shoulder proves otherwise. "No, you're not," he growls. "You're a liar, *Hannah*. I'm done being your little fuck boy. You don't trust me, and I sure as fuck don't trust you. Oh, and just in case 'Liam' doesn't take your ass in, feel free to stay at my place. I certainly don't plan on sleeping in my own bed tonight."

He stalks off, and the pain I feel piercing through my chest shouldn't come as such a shock. Nonetheless, I have to bite my lip to silence another word. The worst part? I can't even blame him.

Or the figure sauntering toward me now, her head held high. Her cold, hard stare warns that she's fully prepared to finish what he started.

"So, just how long have you been fucking him, huh?" Mara demands, her hands on her hips. Several people turn to stare, but she doesn't bother to lower her voice. "He denied it," she adds haughtily. "But he didn't have to. I just wish my so-called friend would have been the one to tell me so that I didn't make an ass of myself, trying to seduce a man who's already taken. I knew you were an ice-cold bitch, Hannah. But that's low, even for you. Why are you even here?" she adds, gesturing around us with a wave of her hand. "It's not like you give a damn about Faith. Or is it because of him?" She jerks her chin in Rafe's direction as he departs. "You're so desperate to stay on his dick, you'll chase after a dead girl? That's sick, Hannah."

"Mara!" I start toward her, but she spins on her heel and marches away, drawing disapproving glances from those on the outskirts of the service.

As the attention turns to me, I set my candle aside and start across the park. Shame sears my eyes with the threat of tears and tightens my throat. Deep down, I know I don't have the right to be upset.

I *am* a liar. One who's gotten so good at it, she fools herself most of all…

"I don't know what you're talking about," comes a voice that freezes me in my tracks, snapping me from my thoughts.

Rafe. His tone is even colder, but I sense that even before I turn in his direction, he isn't talking to me.

However, he's close only a few feet away near a swaying copse of trees—and he isn't alone. A taller man stands across from him, his silhouette stiff and formidable. Even with his face in shadow, I recognize him instantly—Rafe's uncle.

"Don't play games with me, Rafael," he growls. "First, you pussyfoot around our enemies. Then a girl is murdered in our territory, and you do nothing. Fucking seems to appeal to you more than upholding your duty."

Rafe remains rigid. Frozen. I'm too far back to see his face clearly, but I have no trouble picturing it—watchful eyes, terse frown. The way he suddenly shifts reveals even more. He's on edge.

"I don't understand why you're itching for a fight so badly," he says in a tone that rings out firmly. Cautious. "Gino's just a punk—"

"You don't decide that," Shen snarls. "I do. And I think it's time I stop coddling you, the same way I had to stop enabling your father's bad habits."

"What are you saying?"

"I'm saying if you want to play at independence, then fine. Start with repaying Zhang's debt, you can repay me for your little shop as well. Consider yourself financially independent. I'm done bankrolling your ass."

"I earned my money," Rafe says so fiercely my gut clenches in response. He sounds the same way he did when he spoke of his mother. When he swore he was nothing like her. "I've done everything you've asked of me."

"Have you?" Shen cocks his head in a way I can only describe as smug. "I don't think so, boy. You shy away from using force to protect our territory. You balk at anything that might offend your pathetic idea of morality—but you forget. Everything you are, everything you have is because of me. Do you really think you can stand on your own?"

He turns, leaving Rafe to follow.

Which, despite a second of hesitation, he eventually does.

Dread rips through my chest as I watch him go, his shoulders hunched. In contrast, his uncle moves leisurely, radiating confidence in a way that makes me shiver, though I have no idea why.

Several seconds pass before the realization slaps me in the face—he walks the same way Branden does. So sure of his control, he doesn't doubt for a second his hold on the person under his thumb.

Like a predator.

They're barely out of view when another sound catches my ear—a persistent, musical ping. It's coming from my bag, and I reach inside. Instantly, my hand falls over Rafe's phone, the culprit of the noise. It's pinging with incoming messages. I scan them warily, feeling the air leave my chest as I register the topmost one.

Where are you?

From Branden? Somehow, he got ahold of this number, always one step ahead. I whip around, eyeing the shadows. I'm so ready for him to jump out from behind a tree, eager to corner me again. As I open my stance, I try to tell myself I'll fight this time. Scream. Run. Anything but stare and wait. And wait...

CHAPTER ELEVEN

Heart pounding, I look down and realize that the sender's name is already programmed into the phone.

Sexy motherfucker.

Confusion robs my body of tension as another message appears on the screen from that same sender.

Stay at my place tonight, he warns. *Don't be a dumbass. Your "brother" isn't the only asshole looking for you. Gino's been running his mouth. You'll be safe at the shop.*

I swallow hard as a million different emotions hit me all at once. Somehow, I manage to compile a reply, fighting against my shaking fingers. *Where will you stay?*

Wherever the fuck I want, he responds within seconds. *With whoever the fuck I want.*

I clench my jaw, knowing that I'm reacting just how he wants me to. Hurt.

All I can think of to type back is a pathetic plea. Bonnie would make a fitting rebound, but…

Don't use Mara to punish me.

Don't play the victim, he counters. *She's a big girl and can handle herself. But can you? Gino's men won't fall for those bunny eyes. Don't. Be. A. Dumbass.*

He's right—and knowing that stings more than any insult. Sighing, I look up and try to guess my location in relation to his shop. I head there slowly, not out of guilt or a sense of duty. Mainly pure self-preservation and a niggling, selfish impulse that won't let my thumbs leave the cell phone's screen.

Liam is a friend, I find myself typing. The excuses keep coming one after the other, written without any pretty prose —just stark honesty. *I used him to make you jealous. I won't deny that.*

Holy fuck, Rafe snipes, his hostility palpable even through the screen. *Is that the truth? Give the woman a goddamn medal. Now, if you'll excuse me, I aim to be balls deep in some pussy. Preferably one belonging to a bitch without a "Liam."*

Again, I flinch as his barb hits its target.

Beyond the cruelty, I have to admit that I'm impressed by the extent of his vocabulary. In fact, I think he's deliberately trying to provoke me on that front, proving once more that he's not the punk he pretends to be.

So in the spur of the moment, I drop my own guard and copy his tactic.

I express the one thing I don't think he expects from me—the truth.

You scare me, I confess, hitting send before I can rethink the message.

His next reply—if he's preparing one at all—doesn't come right away this time. Tearing my gaze from my phone, I spot a familiar street sign and feel some shred of relief. I'm near his shop already, and I slip into the alley, approaching it from the back instead of the front. It takes me a few seconds of fumbling with his keys before I get the door open and enter his apartment.

When I sink onto the couch, he still hasn't replied. I exchange my clothes for a nightshirt and enter his room, crawling onto the bed.

Still no answer.

Because I do trust you, I add, letting my fingers linger over every letter until I finally hit send.

Judging from how quickly his next reply comes, he's been anticipating as much.

Lying. Fucking around. Treating me like a dirty little secret. Some definition of trust, he says.

While being "balls deep in pussy"? I can't tell. It startles me just how much the prospect stings. Him with someone else. Another woman tracing the swirls of his tattoo with avid interest. Someone else moaning into his ear. Clawing at his back. Someone else in his arms, relishing his heat.

Mara?

Bonnie?

An entirely different woman?

It doesn't matter. In this arena, he's resorting to his preferred weapon of choice—sex.

I don't want to be with Liam, I admit, fully aware of how pathetic continuing this conversation might seem. Someone like Mara would probably block his number and go on with her night. She wouldn't beg.

But Mara never saw the man he is beneath the mask. Even if I wrote off his bravado and swagger, I couldn't escape one glaring image in my head—his face when he saw me with Liam. That rage wasn't faked. Or the pain.

I hurt him.

So I keep typing, even at the expense of my pride. *I don't want you to be my dirty little secret. I want to be with you.*

I see the flashing symbol indicating he's responding in real-time. My breath sticks in my throat, staying there as the seconds pass before the symbol vanishes without another message. For a minute. Longer.

Ironically words are supposed to be my medium. My outlet. My one way of getting my intentions out into the world unfiltered.

But there's no pretty way to spin what I've done to him. No way to wiggle out of this web of lies. In a moment like this, I can only show him.

My heart races as I sit up and strip my shirt without thinking through the consequences. Adrenaline feeds through my blood, but doesn't provide any extra confidence. I'm scared. Niggling paranoia mocks me with all the ways this moment could be violated. Branden could have snuck in somehow and hidden another camera, spying on me from a distance.

It would certainly explain why he hasn't already broken down the door and dragged me back to his home by my hair.

But for the first time in my life, another fear takes precedence over my apprehension of him. It's simple and selfish at its core—I like being free. I relish every minute spent away from him.

And even if he's done with me, I don't want to lose the one person who made this possible. Sucking in a breath, I manipulate the camera to face me and strike the shutter button. A heartbeat later, the resulting image floods the screen.

She's a world apart from Rafe's beautiful, stylistic image.

This figure is one-hundred percent how I see myself. Me. Wide-eyed and unsure, my shirt off, breasts bare. My body exposed.

All of the reasons not to send it race through my mind, forming a mantra of sorts. If anyone could use this against me, it would be him. As blackmail when he grows bored of me. As leverage over my brother and his position as an officer. As pure fodder to feed his stud reputation.

The list goes on and on.

But the more I stare at myself, the more nuances I pick up that I'd overlooked at first. And I come to one startling conclusion—I was wrong. The look in my eyes isn't shame or fear. Instead, it's a mirror image of the one he crafted in his sketch of me.

Guarded. Mysterious—but with a hint of the emotion, he exudes in spades—honesty.

Any doubt I had vanishes as I hit send and slump onto my back, staring up at the ceiling. He could reply with some cruel comment or never at all. He could be fucking Mara or who knows who else.

He could be doing whatever he can to hurt me back. To punish me for lying to him.

I still don't think I'd regret it. For the first time in my life, I caught a glimpse of the Hannah I never see in my own reflection. The woman he's been taunting me with all along.

She's real.

I'm more than some fearful, little bunny.

As the seconds tick by without a response, I'm resigned to the fact that this is all I'll get from him. Maybe I can live with that. Grow from that. Even his rejection would be well worth the new perspective.

There's more to me than cowering, and lies, and fear...

I've barely finished the thought before my screen lights up.

More.

I shiver at that sole command. I can imagine him voicing it against my ear, his voice gruff, breath like fire against my earlobe.

Alight with his encouragement, I reposition myself and raise the camera, aiming lower. This time, I don't have to wait for his reply, brusquely succinct.

More.

Excitement electrifies me in ways I never knew were possible. My brain shies away from the comparison at first —only to cling to it ferociously. It's the same thrill that infects me whenever I write. The inane belief that anything is possible as long as I will it to be. That my actions can shape the universe, for good or bad.

That I have control.

Power.

But for how long? A lump in my throat warns me that I'm standing on the ledge of some massive precipice. One wrong move and a few bruises won't be the outcome—I'll be decimated. At the same time, by taking this leap, I may finally unfurl those damaged, singed wings I've kept suppressed for so long.

It doesn't take long for me to settle on a response. Tumble or fly?

When I finally lower my fingertips to the phone's screen, a part of me knows deep down that he's waiting for it, eyeing his phone avidly. In this moment, I have power over him, whatever that means in the long run. Even if it's for a few, sordid seconds. My words. My images. Me.

I have him.

But there's an alarming realization wrapped up in that reality, one I don't even want to explore in full just yet.

I may have him for now, but...

I don't want to let him go.

Shifting onto my back, I draw my knees up to my chest and take a photo. Then another. Another.

They dance across the screen one by one, each near instantaneously garnering a "seen by" caption. Soon, the indicator that he's writing back flashes at the bottom of the conversation.

Damn head fucker, he says, and even trying to envision his expression makes my belly clench. I can practically hear his groan from here. *Show me what a bunny does when she's very, very sorry.*

Just like that, the tables turn. Yes, I hurt him.

And he's delighting in punishing me.

This time, I slump against the pillows and take a picture of my face, my expression weary. No fake smile. No sensual mask. Just me.

I'm sorry you're with Bonnie and not with me.

I see that he received the message, but there's no reply. Silence stretches on for what feels like an eternity until I finally hear it—the distinctive click of a door opening down below. I bolt upright, torn between the horrific possibility that Gino's men have returned, or an even more terrifying prospect.

That *Rafe* is the one boldly creeping through the lower level. The unsteady figure climbing the stairs with deliberate slowness, each step resonating loud enough for me to track. He's methodical to the point of torture, giving me more than enough time to mull over what his quick arrival means.

That, even if he were still near the park, he started driving here early in our conversation. Maybe before the pictures. The banter. All this time, he was already on his way to me.

My mind is still reeling as the intruder enters the apartment and advances down the hall, creeping ever closer to this room. Then, the door itself opens, revealing a realm of shadow and a figure who dominates the center of it.

Something strikes the floor with a thud, making me jump. His shoe? Then another, followed by a lighter swishing noise. His clothing. He steps forward, allowing me to make out the hint of his motions through the dark.

Gleaming muscle reveals he's already shed his shirt, cording in his forearms as he works on the clasps of his jeans. Unable to tear my gaze away from him, I rise onto my knees, staring avidly as he tugs them down, down, down…

Then he steps forward, robbing me of my view, as his fingers shoot out to trace the line of my jaw. "You want to be with me, huh?" His husky murmur sets my blood on fire.

Before I can answer, he snatches both of my hands, raising them above my head. Under his control, they form an x over my chest as he leans in, shoving me onto my back. Breathless, I can only gape as he nudges my legs apart with his knee.

"Prove it," he goads against my exposed collar. "Prove you want to be with me."

How? He doesn't leave it up to my imagination to figure out. His hands pin me in place as he juts his hips forward, entering me with a desperation that has us both gasping out. Eyelids fluttering, I marvel for the umpteenth time at the fit—the feel of him.

Perfection.

Greedily, I claw at his back, locking my knees around his waist.

And I show him exactly what I want from him.

Everything he has to give.

CHAPTER TWELVE

He doesn't let me sleep; I wake to the sensation of his fingers sliding inside me, wringing a moan from my throat. This round winds up moving into the shower, and by the time we're done, the hot water runs ice-cold.

Afterward, we get dressed—him in a pair of jeans and a black shirt, while I wear a similar shirt but paired with a loose gray skirt of my own.

On his way into the hall, Rafe snatches something from the dresser and holds it out for me to see. His cell phone.

"Watch," he commands before brushing his thumb across the screen, flicking through several images. Each one makes my cheeks grow hotter until I can't even meet his gaze.

But he's persistent, his voice so low the vibration resonates in my bones. "Look."

As my eyes flick up to his hand, he strikes a button, and the current picture vanishes. Then he proceeds to do the same until each one is deleted.

"Give me your phone," he says next.

I find it coiled within the bedsheets. Without hesitation, he does the same on my device, deleting every single picture I sent him last night. When I finally gather the nerve to face him again, he shrugs at my look of confusion. "Those belong to me. Only me."

Meaning he won't hoard them for ammunition later, or so I assume. I'm confident enough to believe he won't share them either. Those intimate pieces of me will dwell within his skull for only him to enjoy—no one else.

When he hands me the phone, I can't take my eyes off the now blank screen. It seems that he's accepted my written apology, but I might as well say it out loud.

"I'm sorry for lying to you," I blurt in a rush. "I'm sorry. There isn't anything between Liam and me. And I'm sorry for putting you in an awkward position with Mara."

His laughter is such a shock, I whirl to face him. He's watching me in return, his lips quirked, his eyes gleaming. "I never thought I'd hear a woman apologize for that," he murmurs, stepping close enough to flick his thumb against my chin. "I'll tell you how you can make it up to me."

"How?" I ask in a whisper.

"From here on out, you tell me everything," he says. "Everything. Like why you were looking at Liam like he'd just punched you in the face."

I stiffen. "That... I was asking him about Faith's case," I admit. "I thought he might know something."

He blinks, his overall expression unnervingly blank. "And?"

"They have a suspect," I confess. "They found Faith's phone and they think that whoever sent her one of the last messages before she vanished might know something about what happened... What's wrong?"

Suddenly, he's staring off into space, his jaw clenched, and a foreboding knot forms in my stomach. After days in his orbit, it's becoming easier to read him.

And know when he's on edge.

"Rafe?" Tentatively, I brush my hand along his shoulder, lingering over his forearm. "What's wrong?"

Finally, without looking at me, he says, "If their suspect was the last person who messaged her, then I know who it is."

His voice is too deep. Too cold. A heavy sense of dread washes over me, but there's no point in running from the truth now. I need to know. "Who?"

I suck in a breath as he meets my gaze in that brutally honest way, holding nothing back.

"It was me," he says. "I messaged her."

CHAPTER THIRTEEN

For what feels like an eternity, all I can do is stare straight ahead, desperately trying to process my emotions. Confusion. Terror. Shock.

He could be a suspect in Faith Wen's murder.

The scariest part? Branden hinted at as much.

Was he lying to hide his own guilt, or is Rafe every bit the criminal Branden's insisted he was from the start?

Turning to face him, I can't tell. He's an enigma, his eyes a stormy black, glowering into the distance. A tiny voice at the back of my mind warns that Branden is right.

I have no idea what he's capable of.

Do I even have what it takes to find out?

"What do you mean?" I ask, taking a steadying breath. My voice shakes anyway, betraying any attempt to sound brave. "Tell me everything."

The look he sends my way doesn't ease my fears one bit. "I'm pretty sure I might be the last one who texted Faith before she went missing," he says. "But I know for a fact that she had two phones."

I feel my brow furrow. "I don't understand. How do you even know that?"

He shrugs, but his eyes maintain that distant, elusive gleam. He's hiding something. "Trust me, I know."

His confidence triggers that niggling sense of jealousy again. I do my best to swat it aside and focus on the information at the forefront. Faith had two phones. A fact that even the police don't seem to know. Liam hadn't mentioned it either.

But why?

"What did you text her about?" I ask, scanning his face for any hint of emotion. Love? Lust? His jaw remains stubbornly fixed, giving me nothing—not that he has to. My brain skips ahead, wondering if they spoke about way more than her problems with Gino and DW. "Why would that make you a suspect?"

"Because I was trying to get her to meet me," he says.

"About?"

His heavy sigh triggers another wave of unease I can't suppress this time.

"Tell me," I prod.

When he finally looks my way, he's more cautious than I think I've ever seen him. Like someone judging whether or not to strike a match over a lit puddle of gasoline. In the end, I guess he has no choice.

"About—" He breaks off, his head swiveling toward the front windows. "Shit."

"What's wrong?" I start to ask, but then I hear it—loud, steady pounding coming from below. The front door?

Above the racket comes a voice, ringing with authority. "Police! Open up, Mr. Wei-Shen. We have a warrant."

Rafe doesn't look anywhere near as shocked as I feel. Without so much as flinching, he grabs my arm and shoves me toward the hallway. From the couch, he snatches my bag and tosses it to me. I drop my phone into my purse before wrestling it over my shoulder

"Get down the fire escape and get to the warehouse," he hisses, already racing for the stairs. "Wait for me there. Go!"

"What..." My brain is slow to process everything at once. All I can do is stupidly ask, "Why are the police here?"

"I said go!" he snaps back without turning around. "Now. Trust me, they won't knock again."

You know why they're here, a part of me whispers. *Because Rafe is their number one suspect.*

Or...

They're here for the same reason Branden hasn't come after me. Because, much like his planted cameras, he's hidden another piece of cruel insurance...

Horrified, I turn to the pile of boxes down the hall and picture the item lurking inside one of them—*the hair clip*.

The muffled chime of the front door snaps me back to the present danger.

"Officer?" Rafe inquires, his voice seeping through the floor. "What the hell is this about?"

"We have a warrant to search the premises," a man replies. I vaguely recognize his voice—the same officer who came the other day about the fire. Judging from the commotion, he didn't come alone this time. I can make out at least four other figures marching in through the shop's entrance. "We'll need access to both the shop and your private residence, Mr. Wei-Shen. We'll try not to make too much of a mess."

From his tone, it's obvious they aren't here on a whim. They're looking for something.

And I think I have a sinking suspicion as to what.

As quietly as I can, I lunge toward the box of my belongings and dive into the first one. Inside is just a random assortment of clothing and books. The second one is no different.

Panic urges me to keep searching as muffled footsteps emanate from the lower level, moving toward the back of the shop with a purpose that leaves no doubt as to where they're headed next.

Gritting my teeth, I double my efforts, ripping through my belongings as quickly as I can. It isn't until I reach the third one that I finally discover my old shoebox of trinkets. I grab the hair clip and wrench open the window just as a cadre of footsteps ascend the staircase.

There isn't time to think or plan. Without barely a glance downward, I scramble onto the windowsill and aim for the fire escape below.

With a heart-stopping thud, my feet land on the rickety structure, which squeals in protest. The sharp noise is loud enough to be heard across town, and I can't stop myself from glancing at the window. If the officers noticed, I only have a second or two to react.

So I move, blindly scrambling to the lower level where a steep drop separates me from the ground. There isn't time to unfurl the nearby ladder. Clutching my bag, I close my eyes and jump instead, landing in a crouch on the pavement.

Staggering upright, I scramble deeper into the alley. Another glance over my shoulder reveals no one is following me—yet.

But a sudden movement from the corner of my eye dashes that hope—it's already too late. Someone grabs my forearm, dragging me around a corner before I can even get my bearings. Alarm shoots down my spine as a familiar smell itches my nostrils.

I know before I even spin around to face him, just who has me.

"Wait," Branden warns in a low tone before I can say a single word. "Don't do something stupid. Just hear me out."

He's not wearing his uniform. Instead, a nondescript black shirt and jeans help him blend into the shadows of the alley. His hair is mussed, his chin coated in fresh stubble. One look at his gaze, and I feel an instinctive impulse too strong to resist.

Run!

"Let go of me!" I tug my arm, discretion be damned. In fact, I should want to bring attention to myself, police or not.

But just as I open my mouth, he tightens his grip.

"Think of your little friend," he warns, dragging me closer to him, his nails gouging at my flesh. "What's her name, huh? Mara Chan? She hangs around the same pieces of shit you do, isn't that right? It would be a damn shame if she wound up like that other girl."

I go limp as my heart pounds. I can't even tell if he means it as a threat or just an observation. It's pathetic how a part of me desperately wants to cling to the latter option.

Even though I know which one is the truth.

"Like 'the other girl.' Like Faith?" I hiss, hating how my voice breaks.

"Hannah..." I'm too slow to cringe from the hand he swipes along my cheek. "I would never hurt you," he says. "All I want to do is protect you. Even if I have to protect you from yourself."

"I didn't hit myself," I point out, swatting his hand away. "I didn't hide cameras in my room, either."

His eyes narrow, unreadable from this angle—but the subtle shifting of his posture sets every nerve in me on red alert.

"Why don't you ask the bastard you're fucking about that, huh? I'm sure he's already bragged to every gangbanger in the city what an easy piece of ass you are—"

I lash out without thinking. My hand harmlessly glances off his chest, but the violence leaves me stunned anyway. I hit him.

And in retaliation, he snatches my wrist so hard I cry out. "What the hell has gotten into you?"

"Who's there?" a voice calls from the direction of the shop.

Hissing under his breath, Branden yanks me deeper into the alley he's in. From behind me, I hear cautious footsteps ring out, creeping in our direction.

They're so close. A scream would be enough to draw their notice. Determined, I opened my mouth...

At the same moment, Branden brings his mouth to my ear. "Do you think he really gives a fuck about you? Hannah, don't be so damn naïve. You think you're the only one he's been fucking? They found the dead girl's phone, Hannah. I'm sure you can guess what was on it?"

I feel my cheeks flush. Rafe told me himself—messages.

But Branden's tone is way too smug to be referring to something strictly platonic in nature.

"Look," he snaps. I crane my neck back despite my better judgment, in time to see him withdraw a handful of crumpled papers from his pocket. At a glance, all I can make out is walls of text. And…

Images. One, in particular, makes me freeze in place—a woman bared from the neck down.

"We need to talk," Branden says, sounding miles away.

You need to scream, the logical part of me warns. Run. But I can't stop staring at the pages in his grasp—those pictures.

They trigger a milieu of different emotions in me, almost too many to explore in full. Disgust. Dread. Familiarity.

But fear wins out. Twisting on my heel, I try to wrench my arm free. "Let go of me—"

"How soon before your little friend gets tossed into a dumpster next?" he warns. "Or even you? I'm trying to help you, Hannah. Fuck! Be quiet."

His hand falls over my mouth, triggering a wave of pain. I squirm, but he only presses harder, his head cocked, his jaw tight. Soon I realize why—a smattering of footsteps echo off the nearby walls, increasingly loud.

"Is anyone there?" the officer questions again, sounding alarmingly close this time.

Cautious footsteps creep toward this part of the alley, and before I know it, Branden's already dragged me further away.

A van parked near the main street is his destination, but I don't recognize it. A rental? Without explaining, he wrenches open the passenger-side door and shoves me forward.

"Get in."

I barely manage to catch myself on the rim of the door. "No." Craning my neck, I hunt for any sign of the officer. If he's still within earshot, he'll hear me. "Help—"

"Fine," Branden warns as the shout leaves my throat. "I didn't want to scare you, but you leave me no choice. You think it's a coincidence that Rafael Wei-Shen went after you?" My expression must give him exactly what he wants —doubt. He laughs coldly, shaking his head. "Oh no, Hannah. I tried to tell you once, but you wouldn't listen— he knows damn well who you are. The fucker's been blackmailing me over it. What? You don't believe me? Here's the proof."

He withdraws that handful of pages and shoves them beneath my nose.

"That same asshole has been talking to the dead girl," he says. "Take a good look, Hannah. This is the kind of monster you let into your bed."

Every ounce of logic I possess warns me not to look, but I'm already scanning the top page, anyway. The exchange reads like a typical correspondence between acquaintances. That is until a series of images creep into the conversation, one by one. The star barely shows her face, but I can guess her identity from her dark hair and pale skin. My chest clenches, my heart pounding with recognition.

Faith.

Whoever she messaged, she sent him images of her face. Her breasts. More…

"You want to know about Rafael Wei-Shen?" Branden taunts as my cheeks catch fire at the sight of every sordid image I come across. "Well, he's had a vendetta against me ever since I busted him for dealing a year ago. He pulled some strings and got off on probation, but he's had it out for me ever since. Enough to set me up for a suspension and fuck my little sister while he was at it. Don't think for a second that he didn't know who you were when he picked you out."

I replay my first meeting with Rafe over and over. The way he looked at me then. How he had singled me out, haunting my footsteps ever since.

Maybe his very first boast to me held the truth all along. *"I want to know what makes a little rabbit like you so damn hard she doesn't flinch when a man presses a knife to her throat."*

All along, he could have known exactly who that monster was…

"You know I'm right, Hannah," Branden says as if reading my mind. "I've always been the only one you can trust. I know you better than anyone."

But the Hannah he's referring to isn't proud or mysterious. She's a world apart from the figure Rafe sees. She pretends to be a captive, but her own lies form the shackles holding her back.

Gritting my teeth, I try to deny it. "You're lying."

"I'm not. The worst part is that you know I'm not. You were dumb enough to think he wanted you, Hannah?" Scoffing, he snatches the pages from me and tightens his grip on my arm. "I'm the only person who will ever care about you. Who has ever cared about you. Now get in the goddamn van."

He shoves me into the seat so hard I lose my balance. Clawing at the door frame, I try to get out, but I'm too slow. Before I know it, he's slamming the door after me, nearly smashing my bag in the process. When I tug on the handle, it's already locked.

My wide-eyed reflection watches me from the window glass, waiting for my next move. But I'm frozen. The panic I know I should feel is dulled by sheer confusion. What was Rafe's real motive if everything Branden says is true? To use me to get back at Branden?

Or use me in another way. Could he have been the one to plant Faith's hair clip after all?

No. I shake my head to banish the doubt and try the door again, fumbling for the button to unlock it. A door does open, but it's the driver's side.

"Don't be stupid," Branden warns as he climbs behind the steering wheel. "We're just going to talk. You're going to listen and give me the respect I deserve. Hell, I'm not just your brother, Hannah. It's always been you and me from the start. Just the two of us, right?" His expression softens as he attempts to touch my arm, but I cringe out of his reach.

"Just the two of us," I croak, pressing myself against my door, as far from him as I can get. "Because you won't let me do anything on my own."

He laughs at the mere idea while turning onto the main street. Then, he rounds another corner so quickly I'm thrown against the dashboard. My wrist smarts as I brace my hands for stability. Amid the hum of the engine, I sense our speed increasing by the second until we're peeling down the streets, heedless of the posted limit.

"On your own?" he parrots nastily. "So that you can keep ruining your life and spewing your lies?"

He cuts in front of another vehicle before darting across an intersection. My stomach lurches, threatening to jump up my throat. "Bran," I croak. "You're going too fast."

God, I can't tell if the last light he passed was even green. All I can do is grip the edge of my seat so tightly my nails bite into the leather. "Slow down!"

"You know," he says in a chillingly calm tone. Without taking his eyes from the road, he wrenches on the wheel, weaving through the thinning traffic. "Liam said something strange the other day. About you."

Pinpricks of alarm bite at my nerves as I race to recall just what he's referring to—Lexi?

He doesn't answer right away. With a shuddering jolt, the van bolts across two lanes, turning onto the highway amid a smattering of honking horns.

I can barely breathe as terror clenches my chest in a vice grip. "Bran!"

"He asked me if 'that' was why I'm so protective of you," he says in that eerie tone. "What happened 'in your past.' He didn't say what," he adds. "But he didn't fucking have to. What did you tell him?"

I choke out an answer without thinking. "N-Nothing."

"Oh? Then why did he have that kicked puppy look on his face? The one that dumb little whores like you inspire by telling lies. What did you tell him?"

He peels down a busy lane, and I scramble to engage my seatbelt. As I shift, something firm stabs against my outer thigh. Alarmed, I swat at it, only to remember the object in my pocket. It's been there all this time.

"Hannah," Branden growls and—despite the chaos of the moment—I marvel at one grim fact. Any other day I'd react to the authority in his tone the way he wants me to. I'd jump. Cower. Confess.

But with Faith's butterfly clip cradled against my palm, I'm reminded of another piece of jewelry. One that Rafe would have no interest in taking.

"Answer me, Hannah," Branden growls. "What. Did. You. Tell. Him?"

"The truth?" I blurt, though I don't know why it comes out as a question. Or it could be a dare. "That you've always looked out for me, haven't you? You've always protected me. And you've always been there to guide me. Control me. Manipulate me. Guilt me into being silent about the things you've made me do. Because it's always my fault, isn't it?"

An emotion flits across his face too quickly to name. His eyes dart from the road for a split second, and the van drifts dangerously toward the oncoming lane.

"Watch out!"

A truck darts out of his path, narrowly avoiding a collision.

"Truth? Don't be ridiculous, Hannah." He throws his head back, laughing. "What are you even talking about?"

"I'm talking about when you made me be friends with Lexi Winacott." It's a strange way to delve into these memories. Like ripping out a knife that's been embedded within me for so long, I've deluded myself into thinking that I'd healed around the intrusion. That I could go on living with the weapon still there, buried deep.

All I had to do was ignore its existence.

But at the same time, I wasn't just protecting myself. Everyone from my parents to the rest of the town drilled into my head that someone else always mattered more.

"She was nice to me," I say softly, watching as the speed dial gauge ticks higher. Higher... For whatever reason, I don't feel the fear anymore. It's as if speaking forms a boundary between my brain and my emotions too thick for anything to puncture. The only way to maintain it is to relive these memories.

Every last one.

"You said you wanted me to have a friend, but that wasn't it." Even back then, he'd kept me isolated, but I had been so desperate for someone to interact with. I'd have done anything. "You had a crush on her. She was pretty—"

"Stop it, Hannah," Branden snaps.

I stare through the windshield, seeing nothing but images of the past. "And you... Dad caught you lurking around the bathroom while I was in the shower. You took pictures of me, then. Polaroids. You kept them in a box in your room, and you always told me that you did it to protect me—"

"You're crazy," he snarls. "Fucking crazy. Do you hear yourself?"

But I do. For the first time in so long, I can finally hear myself speak.

"You told me to be friends with Lexi, and I was. Then you asked me to bring her to the lake, and I did. But you were there... You told me to take a walk." I sound so detached. It's as if I'm narrating a scene from a movie or play—not my own life. "But when I came back…"

"Do you know the damage you could do, spreading those fucking lies?" Branden demands. "Is that what you want? For me to end up in fucking prison because a little liar couldn't keep her goddamn mouth shut?"

"You always made it sound like it was my fault," I say, turning to look at him directly. In profile, he doesn't even resemble the brother I've known. He's a stranger, snarling over the steering wheel. "And I believed you. I believed that everything I did affected you. But that's not the truth, is it? Did… Did you do that to Faith?" I hear myself ask. It's as if my body has taken over, cutting off all input from my brain. "Hurt her because she pushed you away—"

"Why don't you ask your fucking Rafe what happened to Faith?" he demands.

The engine whines as the van lurches forward even faster. Genuine alarm creeps through the numbness, and only now do I realize how tightly I'm gripping my chair. So tight, my knuckles are white.

"Branden, stop—"

"One good fuck, and you already care about him more than me, huh?"

"Look out!"

Another car cuts into his path, and he barely manages to swerve in time to avoid it.

"Slow down!"

"Come home," he counters. "Say you'll do it. Now." He wrenches on the steering wheel, cutting directly into the path of another car.

"Branden—"

"Say it." The engine revs to enforce the threat.

"Slow down!"

He raises his voice to easily drown out mine. "Come home."

We're going too fast. The vehicle sways, fighting to stay in the same lane. Only God knows what the drivers nearby are thinking. Who he's putting at risk.

All of this to make a point.

He's always in control.

"Come home," he goads to reinforce the thought. "Everything will be like it was. All you have to do is come home. Because I'm worried what will happen if you don't. Your friend Rafe thinks he's hot shit, but no one is untouchable, Hannah—and he isn't the one calling the shots. You have no idea what you've stepped into—"

"Then, just tell me!"

"Come home," he insists in a softer tone. "I'll tell you everything if you do. I mean it."

It's easier than ever to sense the lie in his words. I've known him long enough to catch that telltale dip in his inflection. A denial springs to my lips just as another van comes into view.

He speeds up until we're rapidly approaching it, able to see the white stickers plastered on the rear window—a small sticker family, down to a little dog.

"Come home," Branden warns, a dangerous note in his voice. "I mean it, Hannah."

He breaks into the next lane, speeding even more, most likely to cut the other van off.

"Fine," I whisper. "I'll come with you."

"Good." The vehicle gradually slows to a normal speed, and he signals to take the next exit. "This is the best way for everyone," he says. "You've made the right choice."

But my hand is still resting over my pocket, sensing Faith's hair clip beneath.

What choice had she made when it came to him?

And did she pay the ultimate price?

CHAPTER FOURTEEN

The setting sun provides an ominous backdrop of shadow as we pull into the driveway of a scenic, two-story home in the heart of a peaceful, idyllic neighborhood. Children play in the distance, and their laughter is audible even with the van's windows rolled up—a mocking, twisted soundtrack.

"This is where you belong, Hannah," Branden says while shutting off the engine. He braces his hands on the dashboard, his knuckles cracking with tension. "With your family. With me."

An ironic boast, all things considered. This place is a world apart from my crappy apartment or a flat above a tattoo shop. A pale yellow Victorian-style townhouse, guarded—quite literally—by a white picket fence. The imagery symbolizes my childhood perfectly.

A beautiful image when glimpsed from the outside. But what lurks within those four walls? A cage.

I can feel the bars of it closing in as Branden exits the car and circles around to my end, wrenching open the door before I can do so myself. In the same motion, he snatches my wrist and tugs me to my feet.

At the back of my mind, I realize I could always scream. Resist. But I don't. As he hauls me up the front steps, I ask, "So you'll tell me the truth? About everything?"

He shrugs, unlocking the front door. Inside, the narrow foyer opens onto a short hall extending past the living room and into the kitchen. Memories descend, reminding me of how trapped I felt here. How desperately I longed for an escape.

"Honey, is that you?" A blond woman peeks through the doorway, her expression wary.

"Yeah, it's me," Branden says, muscling me forward. The door slams behind us, and I can't disguise how I flinch at the sound. "And Hannah's back like I told you."

"Hey," Kaitlin says with a strained smile. Her blue eyes flit over my posture and linger on my face before drifting away to a painting hanging on the wall. I can only speculate as to what lie Branden told her to explain the bruises. "I'm glad it's you," she says to him with unmistakable relief. "I was worried they had come back and—"

"We'll talk about it later," Branden growls, cutting her off. Just as quickly, he flashes a strained smile and inclines his head down the hall. "Why don't you make us some lunch?"

"Okay." With a terse nod, she scurries into the kitchen while Branden pulls me into the living room, effectively blocking the doorway with his bulk. He meets my gaze, and for the first time, I see a hint of the brother I recognize. The caged, suspicious one willing to do anything to stay in control.

"You promised," I say lamely, but I don't expect a damn thing from him. Mentally, I scan the room, spotting one of the large bay windows overlooking the back garden. It's low enough to jump from.

"I will," he snaps, his voice low. "But first you tell me something. Where is it?"

Real confusion makes me blink. "What are you talking about?"

Belatedly, I sense a telltale weight in my pocket, and the answer becomes obvious. Something small enough to fit within his grasping, flexing hands.

"You know what," he says. Nervous energy seeps through his confident exterior, and he starts to pace, his shoulders hunched. "*You* mentioned a hair clip. So, where is it?"

He eyes my bags, and I instinctively back up a step.

"W-What hair clip—"

"You know what," he growls.

Maybe I do. A certain hair clip that he should have no interest in if Rafe planted it. Perhaps he wants to bring it in as evidence to have him arrested for Faith's murder?

Or…

He wants it for another reason entirely.

"Did you put it with my things on purpose?" I ask, cutting to the chase. At the same time, I inch a step back. Then another.

"Don't play dumb, Hannah." He advances a step, and I sense that distracting him is my only option. If he keeps me here, I suspect I won't ever leave again.

So I choke down any fear and say, "Were you the one seeing Faith?"

He stiffens, his eyes widening.

"You were," I say, taking another step back. "Weren't you? When she went missing, you hid her hair clip. Why?"

I'd assumed he'd wanted to scare me. Threaten me. That everything led back to me—but I was wrong. Foolish.

I can see everything from a different viewpoint now, and the real answer becomes obvious.

"Could it be traced back to you? I know why you were suspended. If something of Faith's could be tracked to you, it would make you their number one suspect, wouldn't it?"

"Shut up! You have no fucking idea how high up this goes. If you keep running your goddamn mouth, he'll come for all of us. I don't even know how they traced her to me—" He breaks off, his eyes cutting wildly around the room. Copying him, I realize why. It's been so long since I've been here that I've missed the scattered cushions thrown haphazardly across the couch. The piles of documents and books scattered among the bookshelves that line the back of the room. Trinkets and knick-knacks clutter the coffee table, and overall, the entire space is a mess.

Which could explain Kaitlin's unease. She had been worried about "them" coming back. Who?

Maybe the same people currently tearing apart Rafe's shop.

"Who will come for us?" I ask, picking up on that one word. How he said it—uttered hoarsely with undeniable terror. "Who are you afraid of?"

"Where is it?" Branden demands, advancing toward me again. I snap to awareness and stumble toward the window.

"You weren't trying to scare me, were you?" I croak. "You were just trying to hide it. Weren't you? Because eventually, the police would come searching for it. Is that why they were here?"

He stiffens, but I don't think he even really heard me. He's too busy fixated on his true aim. "Where the fuck is it, Hannah?"

The hair clip. But if he hid that in advance, then he knew the police would come looking. Meaning anything else that might incriminate him—like a certain series of tapes—must not be in this house either. And then I remember the other unfamiliar object I found among my things.

"Were the tapes on the camera this whole time?"

That catches his attention. He turns around to face me, but I stand firm. For the first time—maybe ever—his glare has no effect on me. I can see through it to the real emotion lurking beneath.

Not concern for me.

Just fear.

"What did you do, Bran?" I ask. "Because whatever it was, it wasn't because of me. Was it?"

His gaze darkens ominously, and I barely catch the moment he surges toward me. I pivot out of his range, tripping into an end table. An array of materials crash to the floor in a jarring cacophony.

"Is everything okay?" Kaitlin calls from the kitchen.

Branden curses under his breath, and I look up to find him alarmingly close, his hand raised inches from my face. "It's fine," he hisses, curling the fingers into a fist.

Soft footsteps start to advance down the hall. "Are you sure, because—"

"Stay in the kitchen, baby." He starts for the doorway and hesitates, obviously torn between threatening me and maintaining his charade. In the end, his façade wins out. He lunges into the hall, hissing at me from over his shoulder, "Stay here. If you leave, I won't protect you anymore, Hannah. I mean it."

I watch him go, and I give myself a second to wallow in the pain. The self-pity. The aching, crushing reality. Those emotions have barely washed over me before a new feeling overrides everything else—the need to run.

I race to the bay window overlooking the backyard. Wrenching it open feels dramatic in so many ways. At least until a set of heavy footsteps approach from the hall. As quietly as I can, I climb onto the ledge and slip through, landing hard beside a hedge.

The noise triggers a flurry of commotion from inside the house, but I don't stop to see if anyone is behind me. I spot the gate leading from the fenced-in yard and tug on the handle. It's locked.

"Hannah!"

At the sound of that voice, I scramble over the waist-high fence in a flurry of motion. Pain lances through my hip, and a ripping sound comes from my skirt as the edge of it catches on a spoke of the fence. Wrenching free, I race down the side of the house. My sandals slam against the pavement as I start running, with no real destination in mind but getting away.

Only when I'm out of Branden's neighborhood, do I finally stop to get my bearings. A series of trees and manicured lawns make up what seems to be a small park. After moving as far from the main road as possible, I adjust my bag's shoulder strap and nearly choke on a sudden realization. Sure enough, I fumble through it and easily find my cell phone.

All this time, I could have called the police—someone else for help.

Could not doing so be written off as fear? Or is the need to protect Branden too ingrained in my being to overcome so easily?

Even now, my fingers shake with indecision as I consider calling one contact in particular. Rafe really was behind those texts for all I know—he even admitted to communicating with Faith.

Trusting him could be running into another trap.

CHAPTER FIFTEEN

A s if to test my resolve, a string of texts flashes across the screen. *Where are you?*

Choking back the doubt, I hit the call button, and it barely rings once.

"Where the hell did you go?" Rafe demands. His voice sounds muffled as if he's speaking far from the receiver. "Where are you?"

I rattle off the street name I spy on the nearest sign, feeling the back of my neck prickle with every step I take.

"I don't know how long I can wait here—"

"I'm already pulling up to you," he replies.

Not even a second later, a black car peels around the corner, skidding to a stop across from my location. I race to it and finally risk looking back.

In my head, I'd imagined Branden chasing after me on foot, always one step behind.

But I don't spy him or his van anywhere.

"What the hell are you doing out here?" Rafe demands, eyeing the residential street with a frown.

I slip inside, locking the door after me. Facing him, I raise an eyebrow. "How did you find me?" Call it a hunch, but I doubt he frequents this part of town.

A harsh sigh betrays his guilt. "Fine." He nods to the cell phone propped against his dashboard. A map is displayed on the screen, with two blinking dots in close vicinity. "I tracked your phone's GPS. Cops show up at my place, and you go missing. What was I supposed to think other than—"

"You thought I had told them something?" I ask, too stunned to feel truly insulted. "Tipped them off?"

He flinches and snatches one of my hands, gripping it tight. "Hell no. I thought some dickhead tried to drag your ass away in the chaos. Was I right?"

I clench my teeth rather than answer him right away. Scanning his expression, I try to picture him on the other end of Faith's messages. Receiving those pictures from her. Asking for them...

"Were you seeing Faith?" I ask bluntly.

He nearly swerves off the road and pulls his hand away to steady the wheel. "Not like that." His tone deepens, fully serious. "I swear it on my fucking mother. I wasn't fucking her if that's what you're asking."

Relief goes to war with doubt until my head spins with the potential outcomes. "I saw the texts," I say lamely.

"I can explain that," he counters, grimacing at the thought. "I was frustrated. She kept giving me the fucking runaround, and all I wanted was—"

"Nude images?" I snap. God, I can't get them out of my head.

But when I finally face him, he doesn't look like someone caught in a lie. Instead, shock displaces any hint of deception.

"What the fuck are you talking about?"

"I saw the messages," I say. "All of them."

He frowns. "Then you saw me cussing her out. That's it. She promised to meet me at my shop but never showed... I should have gone looking for her, but you showed up instead."

I remember that night. He'd been on edge, but I'd been too wrapped up in my own issues to notice.

"So, she never sent you pictures?" I ask.

"No." He risks taking one hand off the wheel to brush my cheek. "It wasn't like that with us, I swear."

"But, the police were looking at your shop for a reason."

"The fuck they were," Rafe hisses. "Luckily, the bastard cops could enact their 'warrant' without me being there. Sons of bitches—"

"Do you know what they're looking for?"

He shrugs. "Anything they can use to pin it on me if I had to take a guess."

He could be lying, but I'm tired of living in doubt.

"I think I know what," I admit, reaching into my pocket. "I think they were there because of me. Because of something I have."

He shoots me a skeptical frown. "What?"

"This." I hold the hair clip up to the light, awed by the detail. Delicate and light, it must have been expensive. Something Faith wouldn't lose easily.

But if Rafe recognizes it, he's an expert actor. His face reveals nothing.

"It's Faith's," I say without beating around the bush. "She was wearing it a few days before she died."

Still, he says nothing. When I gather up the nerve to look at him, he's staring forward, gripping the steering wheel so tightly the car starts to drift and nearly crosses into the oncoming lane.

"Watch out!"

"Shit." He rights the car easily, but his expression is more distant than ever. Even after a few days in his orbit, I can clearly identify the emotion responsible for the tension hardening his jaw. Mistrust.

"How?" he demands finally. "How the hell did you get a hold of that?"

I look at the hair clip again and try to see it how someone like Branden might. Not as a threat meant to terrify me, but as a desperate ploy by someone who probably thought I wouldn't recognize it. Or know who it belonged to.

"Someone planted it in my apartment," I confess. "I think he was trying to hide it in case the police searched his place. I think... I think he hurt Faith, but I don't know why."

The silence between us is deafening. I squirm, feeling my heart race as I try to interpret his reaction. His eyes are dark and thoughtful. Like while this wasn't exactly the plot twist in the narrative he expected, he had been anticipating something similar.

"Your brother?" he asks coldly.

"Yes," I admit. "But now it's my turn to ask a question. Branden Dewitt. Did you know who he was all this time?"

His brows snap together, and he strikes the steering wheel so hard the horn blares. "Branden Dewitt? *That's* who your brother is?" He looks at me so incredulously that I know it's not an act. He didn't know.

"You said his name was Bran," he says, pulling over to the side of the highway. "Though, fuck, I guess I'm the idiot for not putting it together. Branden."

"So, you know who he is?" I ask thickly. "I'm guessing his name wasn't circled on your list by accident?"

He swivels his head to face me. "You want to know the truth? That list was the name of every cop Faith knew had come through Gino's place—but there were about ten different names, and none of them started with D. She wouldn't tell me who was just there looking at tits or who might have been on Gino's payroll."

The irritation in his voice is too real to be faked. "Gino's payroll?" I ask softly.

"I know that fucker's up to something." A muscle in his jaw twitches, his eyes blazing. "Gino's club is a front for something. Faith hinted that it was illegal, but she wouldn't tell me exactly what. I know that it dealt with the girls, though."

"But there's more to it, isn't there? You know him personally?"

He sighs. "When Faith wouldn't give me any straight answers, I decided to get some of my own. I called one of those anonymous tip lines, and the cops actually followed through. They raided the club, but whatever they found wasn't enough to make any arrests. Just get a few unlucky cops who got caught there that night on suspension or some shit. Quietly, of course, as a fucking formality."

Like Branden.

"Let me guess, you've had that this whole fucking time?" Rafe asks, nodding toward the hair clip. "I thought the cops might have been looking for the phone, but that makes sense too."

"Phone?" I suddenly recall what he revealed about Faith having more than one.

"I figured someone would try something to get even," he says, ignoring my question. "Pinning Faith's death on me sure is a start, but it's a damn good ploy. The motherfucker..." He forms a fist and slams it against the steering wheel, making the horn sound a second time.

"Why?" I ask. "I mean how did you know—"

"Faith came to me scared." His tone makes me go silent. I've never seen him like this—posture so tense he's trembling, his lips pursed in thought. "She thought I could pull some strings to get her out from under Gino's thumb. Her parents owed a lot of shit on their house. He gave her the money in exchange for working at his club."

"But you didn't give her the money?"

"No," he admits, his frown deepening. "I didn't. I pressed her for information instead. And when I learned about the asshole she was dealing with... I called in the raid."

"And me?" I can barely get the words out. "You knew my 'boyfriend' was a cop. Is that the real reason why you were interested in me?"

He sighs. "Don't look at me like that. This isn't some fucking soap opera. I was interested in you because I could take one look at you and know there was more to you than some fucking bunny sweater."

"More," I echo. "Like my brother being on the police force?"

I'm holding my breath before I realize it, dreading what he might say. As the seconds tick by in silence, I don't have any other choice but to ask him directly. "Did you want to use me to get to him?"

"And how would I do that, huh?" he demands, raising an eyebrow. "You tell me."

"Manipulate me," I say. "Pump me for information. Use me to get back at him. I don't know—"

"I didn't know he was your brother," he insists. "This whole shit was a lot less creepy when you had a fake boyfriend."

"So, now what?"

"Now?" He inhales, gripping the steering wheel, his gaze determined. "We figure out what the asshole is planning. I don't think the police are at my place just for some fucking hair pin, bunny."

He's right. "You're their suspect."

"I can't even blame them," he says with a cold laugh. "I'd suspect me too. But they're looking in the wrong direction."

"Because Faith had another phone," I finish for him. Another realization dawns on me as I watch him nod. "And you know where it is."

"That night you saw her at my place? She gave it to me then. The phone that matters anyway."

I can clearly recall that moment in his warehouse.

"Why didn't you turn it in?" I ask. "Why didn't you—"

"I'm not turning shit in until I know for sure what's on it," he counters. "I'm not letting anyone whitewash this case."

"So, what did you find?"

He grits his teeth in a rare display of vulnerability. "Nothing. It's locked. Password-protected, and I'm already on my last try. She never actually told me what it is. I thought it might be the guy's name, but DW hasn't worked. Go fucking figure."

I suck in a startled breath. "Is that really why you had the police roster?"

He nods, oblivious to my shock. "Call me Sherlock Holmes, bunny. But DW must be an alias or some shit. Or she was lying about him being a cop at all."

Or 'DW' didn't stand for the culprit's initials in the way he expected.

"Her phone was supposed to hold whatever information she had," he adds. "Don't ask me what. She was vaguer than you when it came to detail."

"Show me?"

I can't describe the way he looks at me. Impressed? Guarded? "You think you can crack it when I couldn't?"

I don't answer. Maybe because if my hunch is correct, it could change everything, the final nail in the coffin.

If I'm right, my life, or my family, will never be the same.

"Bunny?" Rafe prods, nudging my shoulder.

"Just show me," I whisper. I don't sound confident in the slightest. Just resigned.

"I'll take you there. I put it somewhere safe," Rafe says, putting the car back into gear.

Warily, I ask, "Where?"

But I can guess the destination before he even says it out loud.

The one place he seems to frequent even more than his shop.

CHAPTER SIXTEEN

Unsurprisingly, we wind up in the same rundown area as his warehouse. Given the instructions he gave me the day Gino's men attacked him, this place must mean a lot to him.

"Is this your safe house?" I ask though I don't even know if that's the right term.

Apparently not because he laughs as he exits the car. When I copy him, he's still laughing, his eyes gleaming with a hint of something that could be amusement in another setting.

"You've been watching too many cop dramas, bunny," he says. "Come on."

He leads the way inside and switches on a lamp before venturing deeper into the space. From the assembled chaos in the far corner, he withdraws a red toolbox, and I'm reminded of something he told me once before. *"You get there, and you wait for me. If I don't show, you look for a red case. I already changed the combination to something you'll be able to guess…"*

"Here's your trial run," he declares as if sensing my train of thought. He approaches a wooden table in the center of the room and beckons me closer with a crooked finger. Then he slams the case down before me. "If I weren't here, how would you open it? Don't look at me for any hints, either. Use that bunny brain."

I wordlessly accept the challenge and observe the lock in question. It's similar to the kind I used on my high school locker, though instead of numbers, five letters make up the combination.

"Most people use their birthday," I point out, running my finger across the width of the device. "But I don't know yours, and it's not numbers, so…"

"And I'm not most people." He grazes my lower lip with the tip of his thumb, catching me off guard. "Be serious for a minute. If I didn't show the other day and you found this, what would you try?"

I think for a long moment before I finally make my attempt. As I turn to the lock, he pulls away, and I sense his gaze with every move I make. Knowing that, I'm deliberately slow, allowing him to see each symbol I land on before moving on to the next. Finally, as I near the very last letter, the lock clicks open.

"You used bunny," I say softly, eyeing him through my lashes. In a sense, it's humorously cliché, but the seriousness of his gaze belies another reason for the password, other than a joke. The thought ignites a heat that blazes beneath my skin, growing hotter the longer he maintains eye contact.

"I think I have a soft spot for them," he says in a tone that makes me shiver. He's disarming like this, and my body reacts to him in ways I can't deny. Or ignore. More fire creeps into my cheeks, and I glance down, hunting for a distraction. I find one instantly in the form of a slim, pink item resting on the bottom of the box.

Faith's phone.

Rafe starts to power it on, but I grab his hand before he can.

"Won't the police be able to track the GPS?"

He shrugs. "I doubt they know about this one. She only recently got it before she died, and she gave it to me not long after."

Supposedly to give him whatever information she knew— only she never got the chance to provide him with a way to access it.

Could the key really be what I think it is?

My thoughts are still swirling as the phone comes on with a musical jingle. It opens onto a bright pink screen that houses a demand for a password, and I grit my teeth in grim anticipation.

"So let's see it," Rafe says, handing it to me. "Show me how that bunny brain works."

Carefully, I press my fingers against the screen. Even as I type out the series letters, I'm praying that I'm wrong. Every clue leading to this conclusion is just an awful coincidence. I've been wrong all along…

But with a musical ping, the phone unlocks, opening onto an even pinker home screen.

"Shit," Rafe snaps, snatching the phone from me. "How did you—"

"Not yet," I plead, blinking back any tears that might form. "Let's just find out what she was hiding. Please."

He turns his attention to navigating to the sole icon visible on the screen. Once tapped, it opens onto a list of various numbers and letters.

"Are they dates?" I guess attempting to make sense of the data.

"I think so," Rafe says, his eyes narrowing. "Or… GPS coordinates? God damnit, Faith. What were you trying to tell me?"

"Why GPS coordinates?" I ask, seizing on that possibility rather than focusing on the obvious—Branden was DW.

"Could be to stash houses," Rafe suspects, his head cocked. "For whatever Gino is *really* serving at his club."

I swallow at the venom in his tone. "So how do we find where they lead? Google?"

"Probably." He nods, stroking his chin. "But we'd need more than just the locations. Who owns them? What happens around them. That sort of shit. Something specific the police wouldn't be able to ignore."

"Just what do you think Gino is up to?"

"What we need is answers," he says without addressing the question directly. Tucking the phone into his pocket, he starts for the exit. "I think I know how to get them."

His tone triggers a chilling sense of déjà vu. It's the same way he looked right before roping me into a drug deal. Like he's trapped inside an invisible cage with no clear way out but to resort to desperation.

Staggering from around the table, I race to catch up to him. "Meaning…"

"Meaning I know a guy who could give us that information," he says from over his shoulder. "But it wouldn't be cheap."

"How much?"

He scoffs. "A lot more than money. A lot fucking more."

I shiver, hating that my intuition was spot on. "We have to get justice for Faith," I say, even as I inwardly balk at what that might mean for my family. I'm not the only one with something at stake, though. "Especially if you're a suspect."

"Let's go," he says, leading the way from the building. "But don't say I didn't warn you."

OUR DESTINATION GIVES me a horrific flashback to the warehouse we went to for his uncle. Only a few key differences provide any ounce of reassurance—we're still in the city, for one. Though, this desolate street strewn with stray pieces of garbage doesn't instill much confidence, even before I look at Rafe. He's hunched over the steering wheel, wearing the same tense expression he did as he held the gun on the dealer.

Like he's toying with a decision from which there is no turning back.

"Sit tight," he tells me, slipping from the driver's seat. "Give me ten minutes on the fucking dot. I don't come out? You go back to the shop and pretend you were there all fucking night. Got it?"

"No!" I'm already unfastening my seatbelt. To his annoyance, I wrench open my door and place one foot on the pavement. "You don't get to drag people into situations like this with no explanation. *Again.*"

He winces at the reminder. "Fine. The guy here cracks video, phones, laptops. You name it, and he can probably rip into it, among other things. If anyone can help us make use of what info Faith had, he can."

"You don't look very convinced," I point out, eyeing his hands. They're clenched so tightly the knuckles protrude.

"A better option would be going to the police directly, but who knows how many are up Gino's ass? This is the next best thing."

But his tone alone gives me doubt. "Can you trust him?" I ask.

He switches off the car, and muscles open his own door. "He's damn good at what he does. Not to mention, if it's illegal and risky, he doesn't care."

Admittedly, those actions sound just a step below a drug deal.

"The more you elaborate on this plan of yours, the less enthusiastic I feel."

"Look." When we're both out of the car, he grabs my arm, spinning me to face him. "I won't lie to you. It's not ideal, and he's a sneaky son of a bitch. Usually, he wants a favor. A tit for tat sort of thing. He does an illegal favor for you; you do something for him so you can't rat him out. It's why he's lasted in this business for so damn long."

I suck in a steadying breath. "So, is this your way of asking me to cooperate in another drug deal?"

He flinches. "No! This is my way of asking…"

"For what?"

Sighing, he cups my chin, urging me to face him. "I'm asking you to trust me. And I'm asking you point blank— do you want to go in and get involved in that shit? Or wait here like a good little girl?"

I answer him by turning to the nearest building and craning my neck back to observe it in full. "This the place?"

Together, we approach it, following a desolate back road. At a glance, it looks like nothing more than an abandoned brick building. Any windows appear to be boarded up with plywood. An array of colorful graffiti mars nearly every inch of the side sporting a single battered door.

"Last chance to stay out of it," Rafe warns, meeting my gaze. When I say nothing, he sighs again and knocks once. Not even a second later, a voice comes from an unseen speaker.

"What the fuck do you want, Wei-Shen?"

"I'm here for business, Ace," Rafe replies. "Open up."

"You've been banned," the man snarls through the speaker. "Now get the hell out of here."

"Trust me, you won't want to miss this 'business,'" Rafe hisses through gritted teeth. "I promise I won't kick your ass this time. Now, open the damn door."

"I doubt that. Nothing you have could be worth the occupational hazard of working with you."

Rafe raises an eyebrow, inclining his head. "Not even if it could bring down Gino?"

A reply doesn't come for so long I figure we've been ignored after all. I look to Rafe, but he lifts a finger before I can say a word. A second later, I realize what has his attention—

footsteps. They approach sounding muffled as if from the other side of the door.

Then, with a metallic squeal, it opens from the inside amid a muttered curse from a figure I can't make out clearly. He's slender from what I can tell, leaning against the wall of a small, narrow hallway bathed in shadow.

"What kind of business?" he demands.

Rafe wrenches the door open wider and surges inside without an invitation. "Preferably now. So go on and name your price and take me to your little office."

"Hey! You can't just barge in here," the man sputters, attempting to block his path. He's short, with shaggy dark hair and large glasses that make his eyes seem comically wide. Shock doesn't begin to describe what I feel. I'd been steeling myself for someone like Gino or his uncle.

This man, however, doesn't seem to match Rafe's caution.

At all.

"Hey!" he exclaims, barring the hallway with his outstretched arms. "I said, stop! And I don't even know if I should work for you. Not after the last time—"

"Get over it," Rafe snaps, easily pushing past him. "Now cut to the chase. Can you do it or not?"

He's already rounding a corner, and I scamper in his wake as Ace has no choice but to close the door behind us.

"Who is she?" he demands, referring to me.

"No one you need to worry about," Rafe calls back. "Now, answer the question."

I find him in a cluttered room, his arms crossed. I have to blink several times just to make sense of the chaos. It's like a pawn shop exploded. Shelves and mismatched bookcases line nearly every available inch of wall. Each one is filled to the brim with old television sets from various decades, as well as boxes filled with assorted electronics—computers, radios, and pretty much any related device under the sun.

"I'm not doing shit for you without insurance," Ace says, squeezing past me. "Something good enough that if you ever so much as think about touching me, I could bury you."

Rafe forms a fist but doesn't lift it. "Name it."

"You must really want this job done," Ace surmises, a hint of smugness seeping into his tone. He approaches a desk wedged in between two bookshelves and throws himself into the swivel chair before it. A honeycomb of computer monitors, each displaying a different scene, loom behind him.

Swiveling toward Rafe, he steeples his fingers beneath his chin. "What's the job?"

"I need you to crack a phone for me. Every message. Every phone call. And decode some of the information on it." He pulls Faith's phone from his pocket and dangles it by a sparkly pink charm.

Ace raises an eyebrow. "Something tells me that there's more to it than that. So what are you offering for collateral?"

"Scan the security footage from the other night around the west side. You'll catch my car in the vicinity of a drug deal gone wrong. There. You have leverage over me against the police."

"That's it?" The man laughs, throwing his hands into the air. "Petty crime? Oh no, Rafe. I need something more than a tiger showing the same old stripes. Something good, or we're done here. You and your 'friend' can show yourselves out."

Rafe hisses through his teeth. "Like what?"

"I don't know," Ace says, stroking his chin. "Wow me. Something good."

"What about attempted murder?" Rafe says with deliberate malice. "Only it hasn't happened yet."

He takes a step forward, and Ace draws his knees beneath his chin, looking even smaller in comparison. "Hey! Don't touch me—"

"What about a sex tape?" I blurt out.

In hindsight, I have no idea why I brought it up at all. My chest is heaving, my pulse racing, but with every heartbeat, I feel less petrified than I should.

Rafe, however, goes rigid, while Ace scoffs, his mortal peril forgotten.

"With you?" He looks me over and sighs, unfurling his long limbs. "Nice, I'm sure, but not exactly worth my time—"

"Not even if it's Rafe with the sister of a cop?"

"Oh, ho!" Ace sits forward, his grin mischievous. "Now, that sounds interesting."

"No." Rafe grabs my arm, but his touch isn't anywhere near restraining. More protective. A warning. "That's not for sale."

"Too salacious?" Ace wonders, cackling. He spins to face me, stroking his chin. "Tell me more."

Rafe shoots me a warning glance, but I ignore him.

"Would that cover it?" I ask, stepping forward.

Ace continues to spin in his chair, seemingly mulling it over. "This information must be pretty pricey. Maybe I'm lowballing? What else do you have, pretty girl?"

"Take it or leave it, you greedy son of a bitch," Rafe growls. "You have five seconds to decide."

Ace's bravado lasts all of three. "Okay. Okay," he says, raising his hands in surrender. "Give me the phone."

Rafe hands it over, and Ace whirls around to the computer monitors.

"Well, I can tell you one thing," he says after a few moments of typing and navigating various screens. "The GPS coordinates all trace to various locations around the city—"

"Give the man a medal," Rafe says mockingly, clapping his hands. "I could have fucking told you that without playing hacker."

"That's not all," Ace snaps. "Check it out." He prints a sheet of paper that he hands to Rafe. "Read it and weep. Those locations correspond directly to incoming shipments from a supposedly defunct import. The owner's identity is cloaked in a layer of secrecy and obfuscation up the wazoo. Damn, do you know what this means?" A real hint of trepidation seeps into his voice, making Rafe take a step closer.

"Why don't you enlighten us?" he suggests, his irritation apparent.

Ace continues his computer search, switching from various screens to another. Suddenly, he pushes away from the desk so quickly he nearly barrels Rafe over. Spinning to face us, he crosses his arms over his chest. "It means you're in some deep, deep shit, Wei-Shen," he says. "Shit that even a sex tape won't be able to make worth the risk. Our deal is off."

He snatches the phone from the desk and tosses it to Rafe.

"What the hell? You can't—"

"I don't fuck with human trafficking," Ace says, squaring his chin defiantly. "So beat me up if you want to. If you make me go down this rabbit hole, I'm going to the cops. Shit, the FBI would probably be better."

"What are you saying?" I ask, feeling my eyes narrow.

"I'm saying that whoever had that phone was meddling into some deep shit. The information speaks for itself, but don't expect me to spell it out."

I turn to Rafe, and our gazes meet. One look at him and I know he's just as confused as I am. "What the fuck are you talking about?" he demands, speaking to Ace.

The smaller man shakes his head. "Trust me, Wei-Shen. If you know what's good for you, you'll turn tail from this too. Now get out. Now, before you're fucking seen."

He bounds to his feet and ushers us into the hall with a jerk of his chin. "Out."

Rafe doesn't move. "What do you mean human trafficking?"

"You heard me," Ace snaps. "Now get out before I call the police with an anonymous tip about your extracurricular activities."

"Why you little shit—"

"Let's just go," I say, grabbing Rafe by the arm. "Come on."

Surprisingly, he relents to my touch, allowing me to guide him down the hall and out of the building.

Once we're back in his car, he grips the steering wheel tightly, his head bowed. "What the fuck was Faith into?" he demands.

I don't know what to say.

Eventually, he sighs and starts the engine, but he doesn't drive.

"You didn't have to do that," he says in a softer tone, this time speaking to me. "Though it was a damn good bluff considering you don't even know where the recordings are."

"I think they're still on the camera you found," I say.

His eyebrows shoot up, but slowly he nods. "Damn. It's smart, though. But it's a good thing Ace didn't get his hands on whatever is on those tapes. I know he looks harmless, but you have no idea what that motherfucker might have done had you gone through with it."

I face ahead and try not to let my unease show. "Were you worried about me?" I ask him. "Or yourself? Scared of what might happen if Ace got to see you naked?"

He laughs, but his eyes widen as if he's shocked he's doing so at all. "For you, not me. Ace is a goddamn creep. He wouldn't just have leverage over me, and don't doubt for a second that he wouldn't use it over you too. The bastard has no shame. Then again, you do fucking love to play with fire."

He sits back and fingers a lock of my hair, his gaze thoughtful.

We sit in silence for so long, droplets of rain start to splatter the windshield in a quiet cacophony. As thunder rumbles in the distance, I finally gather the nerve to speak again. "I just want to know the truth," I admit. "About Faith. About everything. And if my brother was involved…" I trail off, unable to even finish the sentence out loud. "I want to know the truth," I say instead.

"Do you think you can handle that?" Rafe demands. "Doing what needs to be done, even if your brother is involved. Turning him in?"

"I don't know," I admit, looking down.

"If Faith were just upfront with me, we wouldn't be in this shit. If she trusted me." His voice is a rasp, revealing just how much that bothers him. "Maybe I could have helped her if she did."

"What about her friend?" I ask, picturing the girl we met after Faith went missing. "The one we spoke to in the alley."

"Her?" He strokes his chin with one hand, looking more puzzled than ever. "Maybe… We could—" he breaks off sharply, shaking his head. "Never mind. Forget it. I don't think she knows anything, and…"

I look up to find him watching me, his brow furrowed. "How did you know how to open her phone?" he asks. "You never told me what the password was."

It's a question he has every right to ask, but I cringe in the face of it nonetheless. My eyes burn, watering before I can even think to blink the tears back. In vain, they spill anyway.

"I used DW's real name," I admit. "Who I think he is, anyway."

Slowly, understanding dawns over Rafe's face. His eyes widen, his jaw clenching. Finally, he growls, "Branden *Dewitt*. I'm such a fucking idiot!" He forms a fist, slamming it into the steering wheel, but I brace my hand over his shoulder, sensing the tension coiled within each muscle.

"I think Branden was DW, but I don't think he killed Faith by himself. He mentioned someone. He said someone would come after us. He didn't know how the police had even traced him to Faith—they searched his house too—"

"Did he hurt you?" Rafe grabs my hand, drawing it onto his lap. Heat shoots down my spine as he uncurls every finger, inspecting the small scrapes and scratches I hadn't noticed until now.

"No," I say. "But I'm scared. And if he hurt Faith... He deserves to be punished."

Rafe jerks his chin in agreement. "If Ace is too chickenshit to delve into this, then we need more. Something to tie it all together. We know this 'DW' got Faith into deep shit. All of it ran through Gino's. And now with the fire? His place is ground zero."

"But, I'm guessing Faith didn't leave behind a full confession?" I nod to the phone still in his hand.

"No," he admits. "But I think I know where we can get something close to that."

I raise an eyebrow. "Where?"

"It's a stupid idea," he warns, averting his gaze.

"But it's not like we have a better one. You're a *suspect*," I point out. "We don't have a lot of options. And if Branden—" I can't even say it. The pain is still there, waiting to overwhelm me at any moment. The tears are still falling.

But I choose to focus on what I can change. I'm tired of cowering in my brother's shadow. Sighing, I stroke my thumb across the back of Rafe's hand. "Do you have an idea or not?"

"Everything points back to Gino's club," he says finally, his tone grim. "The motherfucker is hiding something, and if Ace is anywhere near right…then, it's bad. The kind of shit I'd have to be an idiot to get you into. No—" He snatches his hand away, gripping the steering wheel. "I'm not getting you involved in this."

"I want answers as much as you do." I'm surprised by how desperate I sound—and I am in every sense of the word. Desperate for clarity. For the truth. For answers. With a trembling hand, I swipe at my tears and fight to keep my voice steady. "I can't live like this anymore. So tell me what you're thinking."

"Fine," he growls in defeat. "You mentioned Faith's friend—"

"Lylah," I blurt, remembering the name Liam had used. "I think she spoke to the police as well."

"Well, if we can get her or one of the girls still working there to talk to us, maybe they could give us something worth taking to the cops. Something worth dragging Ace by his hair until he gives us everything we need, at least."

I wince in sympathy for the scrawny hacker, but then another thought comes to me. "Wasn't there a fire? Won't it be closed—"

"Like Gino would let that stop him," Rafe remarks with a harsh laugh. "I'm sure he's holed up somewhere. If we could find out where and get in, we could..."

"But Gino would never let you walk through his front door," I point out, envisioning how their last meeting went. For emphasis, I brush my hand along Rafe's still bruised jaw.

"You're right," he says softly, stroking his fingers over mine. "He wouldn't let *me*. But if we could use a decoy..."

"Like me?"

He glowers at the mere idea of it. "Hell no. You clean up nicely and all, bunny, but no. Don't even think about it—"

"I'll do it."

"No." He palms the steering wheel while shifting the car into drive. From the set of his jaw, I can tell that he's more than ready to leave this conversation behind.

But something inside me won't let him balk so easily. "Are you afraid that I'll succeed where you couldn't?"

His shoulders slump in defeat as he shakes his head. "I'm afraid you'll get hurt."

"Then we can do this together," I suggest. "To keep you out of jail and get justice for Faith. Or we sit around and let Gino, and whoever else is behind this, skip away scot-free."

Or allow Branden to get away with murder a second time.

As stubborn as he is, even Rafe scowls at the prospect. "Okay. But first, we need to do some shopping—" he casts a disapproving glance my way. "You won't be needing a sweater where you're going."

I try not to flinch at the ominous tone. Instead, I wipe away the rest of my tears and face forward. "I'm ready."

CHAPTER SEVENTEEN

G ino chose the most uninspired venue to reopen his business—a warehouse just a few blocks down from the original site. We pass the hollow, burned-out shell on our way there. The brick façade is blackened with soot, any entrance cordoned off by a maze of yellow caution tape.

I can't imagine the blaze that caused so much damage— especially considering the residential buildings nearby. Whoever was behind the arson didn't give a damn for anyone who might get in the way.

But why?

"I wouldn't be this sloppy," Rafe remarks, gazing at the destruction in the rearview window as we leave it behind. His hand finds mine with a reassuring squeeze. "If you've changed your mind…"

"No," I say, forcing down a nervous swallow. "I want answers. How did you even find out where the new club is, anyway?"

As if on cue, said building comes into view. Even if he hadn't told me beforehand—judging from the steady stream of people entering and leaving this seemingly isolated place —I could take a guess at what kind of establishment it might contain.

"Ace turned out to be good for something," Rafe says while parking a few blocks down from the club. "I had him track down what other property Gino owned. And guess what? The price wasn't a sex tape."

My cheeks flame at the reminder. "Lucky you."

With sudden seriousness, he braces his hand over my bare knee. His touch is electric, and I grit my teeth at the sensation. I can feel the ridge of every finger, radiating heat.

"You don't have to do this. I mean it, bunny. You may like playing with fire, but this isn't a game."

I have no doubt that he's probably right. But in the grand scheme of everything that's happened with Branden and Faith, I can't ignore a chance to seek out answers. No matter how dangerous it may be to find them.

"It's too late," I say, shouldering my door open. As I step out onto the curb, unease worms its way into my stomach, countering my resolve. Technically, as far as nightclubs are concerned, this is only my third experience entering one.

Faint music emanates from the distant warehouse, audible even this far down. Overall, this is a relatively desolate part of the city, especially compared to Rafe's Dragon's Head venue's busy location. Winding alleys snake through tall brick buildings, most of them seemingly abandoned, making the crowd of people gathered on the next block far more conspicuous.

I'm so caught up in recalling the basics of our plan over and over that I almost forget the presence still beside me.

"I've got your back," Rafe calls from the driver's side of his car, picking up on my unease. "Just keep your phone on you at all fucking times. I'll be listening. The second anything goes wrong, I'm coming in. Remind me again what the goal is."

I sigh before reciting the rigid criteria. An easy feat, considering he's told me at least a million times. "Get in and out. Keep my phone on. Only talk to one of the girls."

"Right," he agrees. "All you're doing is trying to *talk* to one of the girls. Got it?"

"Yes." I start forward, sensing that he's on the verge of attempting to talk me out of it—also for the millionth time.

"By the way, you look sexy," he adds in a low tone that makes me stop short, my cheeks flaming. I look over to find him nodding in approval, biting his lower lip. "You might have to roleplay as a redhead every now and again."

I eye the neckline of the tight black minidress he procured for me. It's the polar opposite of my usual style, along with a wig composed of synthetic curls. A cakey layer of makeup obscures the worst of my bruises, and I'd barely recognized myself in the mirror.

"You have ten minutes," Rafe warns, switching to a more serious baritone. "I mean it. Now set up your phone."

"Okay." I grab my phone from my purse, dial his number, and speak directly into it. "Got it."

Undertaking his role seriously, I sense him trailing in my wake with every step I take. I spy his car lurking a few yards away from the corner of my eye as I approach the front doors where a bouncer stands guard. Tall, bulky, he wears an ill-fitting suit and has a cigarette sticking from his mouth as I submit to his inspection. As Rafe predicted, he takes one look at me and inclines his head to the door.

"Next time, remember that dancers go in through the back," he growls on my way past.

A short, darkened hallway separates the entrance from the club proper. One step inside and I'm bombarded by an arrangement of pulsating, blaring rock music. Blue strobe lights create a chaotic atmosphere similar to the inside of Rafe's club.

The only difference?

The Dragon's Head didn't sport several scantily clad women dancing on various platforms spread throughout. It's such a culture shock. I don't know how to react without giving myself away. Or where to look…

Like a fish out of water, I linger on the outskirts until a flash of a brighter blue draws my attention to a girl walking past. She's tall, thin, and despite the turquoise wig, her features are strikingly familiar. I start to follow her, and something in her posture triggers a memory.

She's the girl Rafe, and I talked to the night Faith went missing, Lylah.

I follow her into a back hallway and then a dingy bathroom that contains only two stalls. In any stakeout movie I've watched, the pursuer would wait and observe before making up a well-thought-out excuse to strike up a conversation—but they had way more time than I do. I figure there's no better way to do this than to take a few shortcuts—I grab her arm on our way in.

Whirling on me, she glowers, her eyes rimmed by a layer of thick eyeshadow. "What the hell?"

"Do you remember me?" I ask. After the whirlwind chaos of the past few days, I'm too exhausted for tact. "I need to talk to you about Faith Wen."

She narrows her eyes, wrenching her arm away. "Who the hell are you?"

"We've met before," I say in a rush. "Does this trigger a memory?"

I reach into my purse and draw out a phone, but it isn't mine.

"Shit." The girl's eyes widen, and she reaches out seemingly by impulse before pulling her hand back halfway. Her trembling bottom lip makes her look far younger than her skimpy black dress would imply. "Where did you—"

"Just tell me what it means. What was Faith trying to expose before she died?"

The girl whips around, glancing over her shoulder as if expecting someone else to come jumping from a stall. "You have no fucking clue, do you?" she hisses. "What kind of shit you've stumbled into."

I grind my teeth helplessly, wishing I had some of Rafe's blunt honesty to draw on. Instead, all I can do is beg. "So help me."

"Fuck off." She storms away, dashing into the main club before I can stop her.

Even faint, I hear a voice issue from my cell phone. "Get out of there, bunny. Now!"

But I can't. Not yet. It could be because of Faith—or sheer curiosity. All of this time, I'd thought Branden's actions were based on me. Because of me. What I did. What I made him do.

But if they weren't, then he had another reason for killing Faith. Another reason for putting her hair pin in a box of my things.

My fearsome, tormentor of a brother was afraid of *someone else* for once.

Who?

And why?

Ignoring Rafe, I stagger down the hall and try to blend in, a surprisingly easy task. There is no main dance floor like Rafe's club. Just a bar, and a series of leather couches positioned around the various stages. As a result, most patrons are gathered around those attractions, leaving the walkways fairly free.

A flash of blue hair catches the corner of my eye, and I surge toward it, spotting the girl darting around a bar counter. "Wait!"

I slip around a scantily dressed dancer, fighting to keep the girl in view. I've barely gone another step when someone grabs my arm from behind, dragging me to a corner booth.

"You think I don't recognize Rafael's little slut?" a man hisses against my ear. "What the fuck are you doing here?"

Terror grips my heart in a vice, and I don't even have to look at him to put a name to that gruff rasp. *Gino.*

I crane my neck back to find him grinning ear to ear, but his eyes are wild. Unsteady. Despite his crisp black suit, instability reeks from him as strongly as a cloying cologne.

"You and I should have a little talk, shouldn't we?" Without giving me the chance to answer, he shoves me against a leather cushion, sliding in beside me.

"About Faith Wen?" I counter, scrambling to put as much distance between us as possible. At a glance, it seems as if we're alone—none of his minions are nearby, at least.

But I don't trust it.

Seated across from me, Gino looks more cartoonish than ever. The club lighting robs most of his features of any definition, and the overall neon blue glow gives him a ghoulish effect. With his teeth bared and eyes narrowed into slits, he's intimidating enough to more than justify Faith's obvious fear of him.

But is he capable of murder?

"What about that little bitch?" he snarls.

I swallow hard, bracing my hands over the circular table between us. Cutting my gaze to the exit, I realize that it would be easy to run. Or grab my cell phone and call for Rafe like anyone with sense would.

But for some reason I'm not even fully aware of, I'm compelled to keep talking. "She was going to expose something about your business," I say bluntly. "Then, she wound up dead."

I marvel at the steady voice issuing from my throat.

Gino, however, sneers at the sound. "Was she, now?" He throws his head back for a loud, barking laugh that has no real amusement in it. Fixing me with a raised eyebrow, he questions, "And what was she going to expose, huh?"

"You tell me," I snap back. "Like…" Glancing around, it's unsettling to realize that many of the dancers resemble Lylah. All are wearing skimpy dresses, and nearly every last one looks too young from the wrong angle. Scared. "Like what kind of business you might be offering other than just lap dances."

Blood rushes through my ears as I belatedly process the dangerous game I've just started—and with an opponent like Gino, who seems to have no trouble breaking into people's property and beating them bloody.

His eyes meet mine with an intensity that warns me he's more than capable of doing worse. So much worse. "Oh, really?" he murmurs. One by one, he cracks his knuckles.

"The p-police are already investigating," I point out, though I find myself eyeing the exit again. The impulse to escape strengthens, and my toes twitch anxiously in their borrowed black heels. "And if anyone else goes missing—"

"Like Faith?" he interjects. His green eyes flit over me as he cocks his head. Whatever impression he has of me makes him scoff. "You really suck at this whole 'Nancy Drew' shit, don't you?"

He slams a hand over the table, so suddenly I jump, but all he does is pointedly flex each finger. "The police, huh? You really think they can do shit?" His cruel smile widens, exaggerating his appearance even more. "Ask your little boyfriend how well the cops around here operate."

But Rafe already told me as much—they're under Gino's thumb. Even Branden admitted as much.

"You want to talk about *Faith*?" Gino says. "Fine. Let's talk, starting with one little question. You look like a smart girl —who do you think led her to Rafael?"

I feel my eyes widen before I can disguise any reaction.

Still smiling, Gino reads me clearly and nods. "Oh, yes, baby. And the dumb motherfucker couldn't even sell me out right." His upper lip curls back from his teeth, his eyes unfocused once more. A part of me shies away from the assessment at first, but there's no way around it now. He's desperate.

And terrified.

"Why?" I ask, more confused than ever. "Were you trying to set him up?"

It would make sense, fitting his cartoon villain persona, but his brow furrows to betray an emotion I least expect. Not smug pride. Just grim irritation.

Hoarsely, I propose another option, "Were you trying to warn him?"

He leans forward, fixing me with a chilling stare. "And if I were?" I can barely hear him above the pulsating rock music —by design, I suspect. His eyes flit around the room, revealing the same paranoia as the girl in the bathroom.

"So you sent Faith to warn Rafe. Why?" I can barely keep the disbelief from my tone. "Why attack him then? Unless you really believe he set the fire."

Any minute, I expect him to laugh or break into some super villain sermon.

Instead, he looks down at his hands, his jaw clenched. "Because some shit isn't worth it. And as much of a pansy fucker Rafael is, I know he's a boy scout. Though, apparently, not a very fucking good one."

Some shit isn't worth it...

"I guess this wasn't all your idea?" I surmise, deliberately skirting naming the topic outright. Again, I keep staring at the various dancers with increasing dread. Despite Gino's confession, I can't ignore the obvious—if he attacks me now, there isn't much I could do to stop him. "Why tell me all of this?"

He lifts his hands tiredly, his smile lopsided, teeth bared. "I'm dead anyway," he says simply. "I'm in this shit too fucking deep. But thanks to your boyfriend, I no longer have a choice."

"Why?" I ask hoarsely. His tone unsettles me more than him attacking me would. Gone is the cocky swagger I'd expect. All that remains is an emotion that eerily mirrors how Branden had looked pacing his living room.

Raw, open helplessness.

"Who are you working for?" I ask.

"Who do you think?" he snarls, practically lunging across the table.

I jump back, scrambling for the end of the booth, but he doesn't make a move to stop me.

"Are you that fucking dumb?" he demands, curling his hands into fists. "I'll give you a hint. Someone who wouldn't want his lackey to know where the real money comes from. Not the same darling nephew who put his own father in prison. Someone with a lot more to fucking lose than me. You mentioned the fire? Ask yourself who benefited from it. Maybe the guy who could spin it as retribution for a dead girl when in reality, he hasn't done a damn thing about it?"

The answer is elusive, and I'm tempted to call his bluff—he's trying to confuse me on purpose. But then something in my brain clicks.

"Rafe's uncle?" I rasp, unable to disguise my shock. "That doesn't make any sense."

"Doesn't it?" With a smug grin, Gino sits back, folding his hands before him. "Rafe plays it as though he's a tough, hard-ass, but deep down, baby? He's a fucking pussy. With him in charge, Shen has a loyal soldier, but one who plays by the rules. Since he's had the reins, the triad has retreated from the game in every sense of the word. What do they do now? Shake down business owners for chump change. There's no real money in that. But Shen knows that no matter how hard he tugs on his little puppy's leash, Rafe won't hesitate to bring him down if he goes too far. The only problem? All the money he funnels into his life, including that nice political run, doesn't come from nowhere."

And maybe he's right. Despite his bravado and tough persona, Rafe had allowed Mr. Zhang to rack up a sizeable debt—only to pay it off himself. That act reveals more than what he made it seem. He'd deliberately avoided extorting the money another way.

Then he took the loss, opening himself up to his uncle's retribution.

"I thought Mr. Shen wanted to keep his hands clean," I blurt, parroting Rafe's own insistence on that fact.

Gino chuckles. "Bullshit. When his precious nephew bailed, Shen just found another fucking patsy."

I don't think he's lying. He's too tense, hunched forward, frustration coiled in his posture.

"You?" I ask, stating the obvious.

He sits forward again, but this time I don't react, even as his breath hits me full in the face. "You have no fucking idea. And if you think me telling you this shit changes anything, then you're wrong. It's already too late, baby. For you, your precious Rafael, and—" He breaks off suddenly, his gaze cutting over my shoulder. "What the hell?"

The back of my neck prickles in warning before I even turn to see why. A tall figure is barreling toward us like a storm, shoving his way through anyone who tries to slow him. In his wake, two bouncers stagger, one clutching his stomach. Only now do I remember the phone in my purse, still relaying everything we've been saying.

And Rafe looks like he's heard every last word. His eyes blaze like fire, his hands curling into fists.

I'm stepping into his path before I realize it, bracing my hand against his chest. "Rafe, don't!"

He easily shrugs me off, heading for the booth where Gino eyes him warily, still seated.

"You think this is funny?" Rafe asks. He forms a fist and punches the table so hard it jolts against the floor, its joints squealing. "Playing fucking games. Spreading this bullshit?"

Gino blinks, his gaze unwavering. "Do I look like I'm laughing, mutt? Maybe it's about time you got your head out of the fucking sand. Look around—" he gestures to the rest of the club with an outstretched hand. "If Shen really gave a shit about some dead girl, do you think he'd let me open up shop so soon? Not unless he needed somewhere to stash his precious pussy—"

"Enough!" Rafe nearly lunges across the table, snatching a fistful of his suit collar. "You work for Shen? Let's call and ask him?"

Gino's eyes practically glow in the dim lighting. "Fuck, yes. Call him, mutt. Ask him why he's cut you out. Made you do his dirty work. The way I hear it, the old man's all but left you for dead."

"Rafe, don't!" I grab the fist he starts to form before he can lift it. Tension ripples off his body like a wall of heat. I grit my teeth in the face of it, and it takes everything I have not to give in to the raw, instinctive need to back away. "Don't do this."

He snatches his arm from me, but in the same moment, grips my wrist as he turns on his heel. I have no choice but to follow him. When I look back, Gino is watching us, his arms crossed, lips still quirked.

And his warning seems more ominous than ever.

"Run little mutt," he calls. "But you know the truth, don't you? You never meant shit to him, and still don't."

Rafe tightens his grip on me rather than answer. As we pass the bouncers, they let us go without a word, and his car is already parked directly out front.

"I thought we had a deal, huh?" he snarls once we're inside it. "Ten minutes, and if I say you bail, you bail."

"I don't think Gino killed Faith," I blurt in a rush. "But he knows who did. I think he's afraid of them."

I hesitate to admit anything more, gauging his reaction. He's staring straight ahead, still furious. Would he even believe that his uncle was capable of such crimes? Though perhaps he'd deluded himself like I had.

But the truth is inescapable. Branden's reasons were well beyond trying to intimidate me.

The silence between us extends as Rafe says nothing, but he doesn't have to. He heard Gino's tirade himself through my phone. Even knowing that I can't bring myself to name the prime suspect out loud.

But I don't have to.

"No," Rafe says, starting the car. "No. He wouldn't... He wouldn't. Not him."

His uncle.

2

I THOUGHT I knew what it felt like to be helpless—but this moment somehow tops any other.

Watching Rafe pace his kitchen, his hands clenched into fists, his head bowed. "No," he growls for the countless time. "No. My uncle may be an asshole, but… No. No. He wouldn't be into that shit. He wouldn't. And Gino? The motherfucker's been gunning for me since day one. He's just fucking with my head."

He has a point—but I can see the situation from a different angle. That of a man who desires only control, willing to do whatever it takes to exert it over his nephew. Like, goad him into a gang war for seemingly no benefit.

Or beat him.

Force him to commit a crime.

Torment him.

"If you went after Gino directly, what would happen, hypothetically speaking?" I ask, picking the less volatile topic to start with.

"Nothing good," Rafe says bluntly. He sighs, bracing his hip against a counter, his gaze distant. "It would escalate fast. Besides, Gino's territory isn't worth the risk."

"Why?"

"We'd have to muscle into his business. You can't rely on sheer force to accomplish something like that. You need allies."

"Allies that your uncle can't associate with if he's supposedly 'clean,'" I say.

He swivels toward me. "What the fuck are you getting at?"

I flinch, but I don't cower. Meeting his gaze, I say, "I think he's been lying to you. I think he's the one pulling Gino's strings, and I think he's about to do something worse."

Something so bad that even Gino was alarmed by it.

But...as his expression transforms into a grim frown, I come to a startling realization.

"You knew," I say quietly.

"I *knew* he could be a petty son of a bitch," he corrects. "So, what are you getting at? He used Gino to run his titty bar?"

I sense it's better not to say anything. Whatever he's going through is personal. A dilemma that no one else can unravel but him.

The same way I have to face my brother's part in this scheme.

"So what?" he demands, though I suspect he's speaking to himself more than me. "He dabbles in human trafficking now? He wouldn't. Why?"

He glares at the wall as if it might give him an answer. A muscle in his jaw quivers and I can almost see the struggle taking place in his brain between logic and loyalty.

"Rafe…" I finally step forward, placing my hand on his shoulder.

"Don't." He shrugs me off, crossing over to the couch. "I don't need you to look at me with those bunny eyes right now. I need…"

"Answers," I say, finishing for him.

"Damn right." He inclines his head, fixing me with a cold stare. "Let's start with the obvious. Your brother's name unlocked Faith's phone. Don't tell me that's a coincidence."

Tears burn behind my eyes, and I don't even try to keep them from falling. Nodding, I cross over to sit beside him.

"It wouldn't be the first time," I admit, hating the way my throat tightens. I've kept these secrets in for so long…

But in a hoarse whisper, I finally spill them. I tell him about Lexi. Her death. The bracelet.

When I finally finish, Rafe is glowering at the floor, his jaw clenched, expression unreadable. I can't move, sick with anticipation of how he might react.

In disgust?

Horror?

"Shit," he hisses, grasping my hand. I go limp to find there is no judgment in his touch. No hate. Only warmth emanating from his fingers, radiating reassurance.

And my head swims with relief.

"I think he may have hurt Faith," I say.

"Look at me." Honed with intensity, his eyes bore into mine. "Were you going to let him get away with murder if he did do it?"

"No!" I say. But my voice sounds flat, even to me. I've let Branden get away with so much. And why? For one pathetic reason. "I thought... I thought it was my fault."

Rafe scoffs. "Because he's fucking brainwashed you."

I don't counter that. "But I don't think he was working alone."

He stands, crossing to the window. Watching him from this angle, I can fully appreciate his strength in every sense of the word. His size, his muscle, and namely his ability to think critically. To push through his own rage and betrayal and see the truth at the heart of the matter.

"Fine. So Shen's dirty," he says, glaring at the street below. "What do we do about it? He must have the cops in his back pocket."

"Not all of them," I say quickly. One person, in particular, comes to mind.

Rafe fixes me with a raised eyebrow. "Let me guess," he says. "Your fake boyfriend?"

I try to ignore his obvious hostility. "I think he learned the truth about Bran too. Maybe he can reach out to someone else in the department? Someone your uncle doesn't control."

"It's dumb," Rafe says bluntly. "It probably doesn't have a chance in hell of working. But we don't have any better options. And… I trust you."

I shiver at the heat in his voice, but I don't allow myself the chance to decipher it. Instead, I fish through my bag and grab Liam's business card.

With a harsh exhale, Rafe snatches it from me, withdrawing his own phone from his pocket. "We have nothing left to lose."

CHAPTER EIGHTEEN

"There are about a million reasons why I shouldn't even be here right now," Liam says, warily eyeing the drawings hanging on the walls of Rafe's shop. I doubt he can see much, considering the lights are off—a detail Rafe insisted on to avoid anyone from the outside being able to look in.

Another precaution is Liam's lack of a uniform. A nondescript sweatshirt instead helps him blend into the shadows.

But his presence here at all is jarring regardless.

"What is this about?" he asks, finally looking from me to Rafe. All I can make out are the whites of his eyes and the firm set to his jaw.

Was calling him here a mistake? Even so, it's not like we have any better options. Taking a deep breath, I decide to forgo any pretense. "Before, in front of the café... You were trying to tell me something about Branden." I hesitate before adding, "I want to know."

Liam's silent. Even with part of his face illuminated by the glow cast by an outside streetlight, he's unreadable. Doubt creeps in with every passing second, and sweat is beading at the nape of my neck by the time he finally sighs.

"I think you should tell me exactly why I'm here before I jump to the wrong conclusion." He cuts his gaze to Rafe, who is lurking near the hallway, his arms crossed guardedly.

Before I can open my mouth, Rafe steps forward. "Lee Wei-Shen," he says gruffly. "Does that name ring a bell?"

Liam cocks his head toward the window, and the extra light reveals his raised eyebrow. "Your uncle? What is this about?"

"Tell me the truth," I say, taking a step closer to him. "You can trust us."

"You go first," Liam counters, turning to me. "Tell me about your brother. The truth." The hardness in his tone warns that he has one topic in mind.

And there's no point in running from it any longer.

I tell him everything. Lexi. Faith. The rest. At the back of my mind, I hate how it sounds out loud, not to mention the risk may not be worth it at all. But when I finish, Liam looks anything but surprised.

"He's been under investigation for months," he admits. "I didn't know about the Winacott case, but there has been suspicion regarding him and corruption stretching back at least a year. However, there's been no solid evidence yet."

Dread congeals in my stomach, as painful as jagged shards of glass. It takes me several tries to form a coherent reply. "What can we do?"

"And how do we know your boss isn't dirty too?" Rafe pitches in. I flinch at the hostility in his tone, but Liam doesn't seem to take it to heart.

He meets my gaze directly, his eyes gleaming in the dark. "Because I'm not really a member of the police." Before the shock can fully set in, he says, "I'm with the FBI."

Rafe hisses. "I hope that's a joke."

"This area has been under surveillance for a long time," Liam says without addressing him. "But we need proof. At least a confession on tape, and I shouldn't have to say that consorting with a suspect's sister and a local criminal wouldn't be cleared by my higher-ups."

"I'm guessing Branden doesn't know, either," I croak.

Liam nods. "Look, if this information gets out, it won't be corroborated by my department, but we suspect some officers have been participating in illegal activities involving a local club and one Lee Wei-Shen." He nods pointedly toward Rafe. "That same club is at the center of a parallel special victims investigation involving suspected human trafficking. Again, we've yet to find any solid proof."

"How the fuck do we get that?" Rafe demands. "Ask him nicely?"

"Or I could," I blurt without thinking the plan through. "I could be the one wearing a wire."

"No," Liam says. "This isn't a TV show. I shouldn't have to tell you that involving civilians would never be approved by my superiors."

Rafe scoffs. "Well, you can give them this." He approaches the counter, placing an object on it. Even in the dim lighting, I can make out its shape. "That's Faith's phone," he adds. "We think she hid GPS coordinates on it. Maybe your 'superiors' can find something useful on it."

Liam nods. "It's a start."

But I can sense what he doesn't say out loud. "But it isn't enough."

"It could take weeks to analyze—which is good for supplementary information, but we suspect that Lee Wei-Shen will make a move soon. Either to liquidate his assets entirely or cast suspicion somewhere else to cover his tracks."

Which would explain why Gino was so shaken.

"He's just one player among many," Liam explains. "This ring stretches nationwide, but we've never been able to crack any of the cells."

"And yet you keep shooting down any suggestions," Rafe points out, his suspicion obvious. "So what do you propose,

Mr. FBI? Though hell, you could be up Shen's ass like the rest of them."

"I could," Liam admits. "And while I can't authorize you to wear a wire and garner a confession on audio—or better yet, catch Shen in the process of covering his tracks—that would be the best piece of evidence I could use to quickly advance the investigation far enough to make an arrest. But it's dangerous." He faces me directly, and for the first time, a hint of concern displaces his otherwise serious expression.

"You said the force here is corrupt," Rafe says, but I don't miss how he moves to my side. His hand lands over my shoulder, anchoring me to him. "My place was searched the other fucking day. I don't think that's a coincidence."

"Branden's was too," I add, frowning.

"If anything were found, there would be an arrest by now," Liam says. "We're at the end of the rope. A few more days without a solid lead, and this ring just moves to another city."

"So, what do we do?"

Rafe inclines his head. "If you won't 'sanction' anything, then what good are you?" he demands.

"I can analyze the cell phone, for one," Liam says, reaching for the device. "And, while I can't participate in any official capacity, I can be on standby. And if I happen to misplace some equipment in the meantime, then so be it."

"Good," Rafe says, his teeth flashing in the shadow. "I have an idea."

CHAPTER NINETEEN

Despite the time I've spent away, Mr. Zhang's shop feels the same. Here, amongst the dusty bookshelves, I can ignore the rest of reality. I even volunteer to finish out the business day, allowing Mr. Zhang to leave early.

But I can't ignore the tension lacing the air with every passing second. I'm jumping at every noise to break the quiet, and when the bell above the door chimes, I stiffen in anticipation even before I turn to face the figure standing near the entrance.

Shock hits me like a punch, but not in the way I've been expecting. "Mara?"

I stagger around the counter to meet her, stopping a few feet away. She's wearing her black uniform from the restaurant and must have just gotten off. Her arms are crossed, her gaze wary.

"What are you doing here?" I ask, but I can't stop myself from scanning the view of the street behind her. Apart from a few pedestrians, no one else is there.

"I'm sorry, were you expecting your boyfriend?" Mara asks, turning on her heel. "Let me just leave, then—"

"Wait! I'm sorry," I blurt in a rush. Awkwardly, I fiddle with a stand of pens beside the register, unsure of what else to do with my hands. From over my shoulder, I say, "I am just surprised you're here."

"My dad needed me to pick up a cookbook for him," she snaps, crossing over to a section of glossy new recipe books. She grabs one seemingly at random and flips through it, her back to me. After a second, she pointedly clears her throat. "Isn't this the part where you grovel for forgiveness?"

"Um…" I blink in shock and promptly knock over a row of silver ballpoints. I scramble to rearrange them, but when I finally face her, she's watching me, her head cocked expectantly. "Yes. I'm so sorry—"

"Good." She sets the book aside and places her hands on her hips. "Holding grudges can give you wrinkles, and I just don't have the energy to expend on dumb boy drama. Besides, it looks like you have more than enough of that for the both of us," she adds, raising an eyebrow.

My cheeks catch fire. Only God knows what the chaos outside of the café looked like to her. "It wasn't like that."

"So what was it like, then? Just you gloating over the fact that you were screwing Rafe despite encouraging me to go after him? That's fucked up."

I don't deny it. Finally, she sighs.

"The least you can do is spill the drama. I might be able to forgive you for keeping Rafe your naughty secret, but two sexy men? Who was that boy scout?"

I choke out a sound that might be a laugh. "Someone who I can assure you is all yours."

"I'm off this weekend," she says, heading toward the door without the cookbook. "You owe me dinner. My parents' place, and you might want to borrow lover boy's wallet. I plan on eating big."

"Deal."

I watch her go, feeling a weight lift off my shoulders. The relief lightens some of the heavy mood from before. When I finally finish my shift and head out the dread returns. I've barely put the key in the lock when I sense a presence approach me from behind. "You think this is funny?" a man snarls against my ear. Alarm shoots down my spine, but before I can even think to run, he snatches my forearm in a vice grip. "You go and jump out of a fucking window? What the hell has gotten into you?"

I turn to face him, steeling myself for what I might find—but nothing could prepare me for this. Branden, but in a state I've never seen him in before. His eyes are wild, hair mussed, and unkempt. Instead of his uniform, he wears crumpled sweats and a T-shirt, and his breath sears my nostrils, unmistakably tainted with alcohol.

"Why are you here?" I ask.

His eyes narrow. "You really want to 'talk'? Then come with me. Now."

He tugs me after him, but I don't resist, letting him shove me into a nearby van. It's the same one from before, and he instantly engages the locks.

I don't bother to hide the fear from my voice. "What do you want?" Fighting to keep my breathing steady, I crane my neck to watch him. "Where are we going?"

"Somewhere where you can't run away," he warns, pulling away from the curb. "So you want to talk? Who have you been running your mouth to, huh?"

His inflection varies wildly, his eyes unfocused as they dart around the road.

Inhaling deeply, I pose a question of my own. "Did you hurt Faith? Were you the one she was really messaging?"

He snorts out a harsh laugh, his nostrils flaring. "That little cunt. Why would I be speaking to her, huh? You ask yourself that."

But the answer is obvious in the way Faith had reacted to the topic of her mysterious DW. She was terrified of him, and I'd been so stupid not to recognize it. The last time I saw her alive, her haunted expression stuck with me for a reason—it was the same exact one I saw every day in the mirror.

"She was someone you could control," I hoarsely point out. "Until you couldn't anymore."

"You think you're so damn smart, huh?" he hisses through his teeth. "You tell me something. Where is the fucking hair clip? Where did you put it?"

I keep my hands in view, neither confirming nor denying that I have it. "Did you hide it in my apartment on purpose?"

"Don't play with me!" He slams his fist over the steering wheel so hard the horn sounds. Wild-eyed, he scans the road, his knuckles protruding from how tight his grip becomes. "Where is it?"

"You recognized her at the restaurant, didn't you?" I say, recalling that night and how angry he'd been. I'd assumed that I was the source of that rage, but someone else would pay the price in reality—just like with Lexi.

And me. My face still smarts if I focus on it. Absently, I trace the bottom of my lip, observing him from the corner of my eye. His expression isn't far from the fearsome snarl he wore the night he attacked me, and a grim sense of recognition strengthens my resolve.

"Did you follow her when I left? Is that when you killed her—"

"You don't have any fucking idea of what you've gotten into. Do you? No fucking idea. Now I have to fix it just to make sure you don't wind up—" He stiffens, and an emotion flits across his face that I recognize instantly. Fear.

A buzzing noise gives me a clue as to why. A ringtone?

"Shit." He fumbles through his pocket, withdrawing a cell phone. "Dewitt. Are you following me?" Whoever he's speaking to says something that makes him glance over his shoulder. "Where do you need me to go?"

He hangs up, shoving the phone into his pocket, and I sense the mood shift as drastically as if the temperature dropped several degrees. Branden, without his cocky swagger, is a stranger to me. He's shades paler, practically glowing in the dark. A sheen of sweat glints off his brow, and I know the alcohol stench isn't a coincidence.

"Who was that? Where are we going?" I demand as he swerves around a corner. "Tell me!"

"Shut up," he hisses. "Just shut up! You have no idea what kind of shit I'm in. No clue!"

"So tell me," I say, scrambling for my seatbelt as the van picks up speed. "Are you working for Lee Wei-Shen? Is that why you hid Faith's hair clip in my things."

He whips around to face me, so suddenly, the entire van jolts with the movement. "What the hell are you talking about?"

"Did you kill Faith?"

Shaking his head, he looks to the windshield. "You think you know everything, huh? Do you have any idea what I've done for you? The shit I've had to do to protect you? But it's too late now—" He releases a harsh bark of laughter that chills me to the core. "He won't let you off anymore."

"He?"

"I tried to warn you, but you couldn't fucking listen! You had to poke your damn nose into everything, didn't you?" He sounds hysterical, and I can't ignore a growing sense of alarm that has me digging my nails into my palms.

"What do you mean?"

He doesn't answer, still laughing maniacally, seemingly too distracted to even keep his eyes on the road. We barrel through an intersection, missing any oncoming traffic by a miracle. Logic warns me to shut up, save the questioning for when our lives literally aren't on the line. But fear and curiosity override anything else. "How long have you worked for him?" I ask, failing to keep my voice steady. It breaks, but I keep speaking, raising my voice until he flinches. "Why? Is that why you had to kill Faith? She found out about what really goes on at Gino's club—"

"Shut up!" The car comes to a sudden stop, and I'm thrown forward so violently my seatbelt cinches my chest. Dazed, I brace my hands over the dashboard and look up. We're in an unfamiliar part of town, far from any main street.

"Just shut up," Branden warns as he climbs out, circling to my end. He grabs my wrist, yanking me from my seat. "I'm warning you, Hannah. This isn't a fucking game. Now, where is the fucking hair clip?" he demands. "Give it to me!"

"I don't have it," I insist.

"Oh, really?" He grabs my bag, wrenching it from my grasp. He rummages through it and tosses it aside. "No!" He warns the second I take a step toward it. "Come on."

His nails rip into my shoulder as he shoves me forward, toward a narrow alley that cuts between two nearby buildings. Dark windows and abundant graffiti allude to them being abandoned, and my breaths quicken, my throat tight.

"Where are we?"

"Shut up," Branden snarls, pushing me forward. Eventually, we reach a battered door leading to one of the buildings. It's dank inside, the air so thick I can taste it. Coppery, like metal. Rust. Wet.

My steps falter, but Branden shoves me further down what appears to be a narrow hall. The pitch darkness is broken only by a faint glow emanating from a doorway up ahead. When we reach it, Branden forces me inside—a wide space littered with wooden crates. A row of large, dusty windows allows some of the outside light in, but it's barely enough to make out Branden's grim frown.

"Just stay here," he says, raking his hands through his hair. "Fuck! Let me handle this."

"Handle what?" I ask. "What's going on, Bran? Where are we?"

He doesn't answer.

The sound of a door opening makes him stiffen, and another man enters the room, his shape recognizable instantly. He looms against the narrow doorway, casting a shadow that seems to encompass everything in its path. But he isn't alone. Someone stands beside him, only his outline visible in the darkness.

Even Branden seems to shrink, whirling to face the newcomers. "I did what you said," he stammers, displaying an unease that shakes me to my core. "Everything. Now—"

"I didn't think you would be this foolish," Shen says, his voice a deep, unsettling rasp. "First, you get sloppy. Then careless, and now you seem determined to amplify your fucking mess."

Branden stiffens. "No! You don't understand—"

"I understand that you stepped right into a trap," Shen says. "And you brought a viper right into our midst—" He nods to me. "She's wearing a wire."

"N-No…" Branden turns to me, his gaze flashing. He grabs my hand, eyeing me with a ruthless flick of his gaze. "I took her bag. She wouldn't…"

"Search her," Shen commands.

I stagger back, but I'm not anywhere near quick enough. Branden snatches my wrist, tugging at my sweater with his free hand. "I don't feel anything," he declares after a moment.

But Shen steps forward, his head cocked. "Then you didn't search hard enough," he growls. "Luckily, I was alerted to your stupidity beforehand."

The man behind him enters the room fully, allowing the dim lighting to cast him in faint relief. At the sight of a familiar pair of dark eyes, I suck in a breath.

"Rafe?"

His gaze is fixed straight ahead, his expression unreadable.

"You can consider our arrangement over," Shen says to Branden, his upper lip curled in disgust.

"What the hell do you mean?" Branden demands. "I did everything you fucking asked!"

"You were sloppy," Shen snarls. "And now I'm forced to clean up your mess. Rafael."

On cue, Rafe steps forward, withdrawing something from his coat pocket. It's small enough to fit the curve of his palm, aimed straight ahead—and its purpose is undeniable.

Branden pales, backing up so clumsily he nearly trips over his own feet. "What the fuck?"

"To clean up your mess with the Wen girl, I have to take matters into my own hands."

"You told me to do it!" Branden shouts, clenching his hands at his sides.

"I told you to toy with the merchandise?" Shen growls. "I told you to run your mouth to that little bitch? Enough of this. Now you have another girl's death to answer for." His dark eyes cut toward me, devoid of any emotion.

"No," Branden growls. "Leave her out of this—"

"You don't have a say anymore," Shen says with a cold laugh. "As far as the police will know, you killed her to cover your tracks. Overcome with guilt, you then turned the gun on yourself. Rafael." He inclines his head toward Branden before turning on his heel to exit the room. "Clean this mess."

Rafe raises the gun, and the world slows to a crawl. I see his face. Those beautiful, unfathomable eyes narrowed with focus. Suddenly, he pivots, aiming in an entirely different direction.

"Don't move," he warns.

Shen stops short, glancing over his shoulder. It seems to take him a full second to realize just where Rafe is aiming. Anger colors his cheeks, his eyes narrowing. "What the hell are you doing?"

"Don't move," Rafe repeats, his voice steady. "I won't ask again."

Shen laughs, an eyebrow cocked in amusement more than alarm. "Don't tell me you've grown a pair, boy?" he taunts. "Put that toy away before you hurt yourself—"

"You really think I'm that dumb, don't you?" I can't even begin to classify Rafe's tone. My stomach clenches at the low, harsh notes roughening his baritone, even as his face remains expressionless. "*That* stupid," he adds. "That afraid of you that I wouldn't catch on. What the fuck was I to you, huh? A patsy? A fall guy?"

"Family," Shen growls, his eyes flashing. "But I suppose I should have known from the time you were a goddamn child how little that means to you. My brother may have shacked up with a worthless whore, but you are his real failure."

"Like he was so great, huh?" Rafe takes a step forward, still training the gun over his uncle's back—but his grip seems steadier. Determined. "I spent my life thinking I had to make up for his mistakes—but that was my real 'failure.' Thinking I owed your ass anything. You don't give a fuck about him, and you certainly don't give a fuck about me."

The other man whirls around, his face reddening with fury. "You think you have what it takes, Rafael? Do it then. Shoot me. Do it!" He holds out his arms, his smile feral.

Rafe doesn't move an inch, but I can feel his anger from here, radiating off him like a furnace. His eyes blaze with an intensity to match the creature inked on his back. When his fingers twitch, I step forward. "Don't—"

"Hannah!" Branden grabs my arm, yanking me back, but Rafe's eyes flicker in our direction. I swear I see him nod once—*I'm okay.*

But Shen just laughs. "You can't even betray me right," he declares, turning for the door again. "I... What the fuck?"

His gaze is directed at something beyond the doorway, but what has him so startled quickly becomes apparent. Footsteps—belonging to several people, racing in our direction all at once.

Loud, a voice rings out, stern with authority. "FBI! Hands in the air!"

I comply automatically, backing up against the far wall as several figures stream into the space. From their posture alone—and the navy jackets with a blazing emblem emblazoned on the front—their identities are obvious—FBI agents.

A slim figure I recognize as Liam spearheads the group, his focus purely on Shen.

"Lee Wei-Shen," he declares. "You're under arrest for suspicion of blackmail, extortion, and conspiracy to commit murder. You have the right to..."

My own thudding heartbeat drowns him out, surging through my ears as I watch two agents wrestle Branden to the ground. One of them pulls out a pair of handcuffs, applying them swiftly.

"Don't look," someone warns near my ear, his voice soft. Before I know it, Rafe is blocking my view, his hands on my waist as my cheek settles against his chest. "Just hold on to me."

And I do, gripping him so tightly my fingers ache. Adrenaline leaves me in a rush, and I'm forced to cling to him, trusting him to support my weight, which he does without a shred of hesitation.

I eye him through my lashes and wince in sympathy. He looks worse than ever, his bruising apparent even in the dim lighting. Carefully I stroke my fingers over the unmarred skin along his jaw, letting the sight distract me from everything else.

And somehow…

It does.

CHAPTER TWENTY

I f I were to write my essay for the Fenwick program now, I know exactly what I'd center it around. *Fear*, the most insurmountable of inner demons. For so long, I've let it choke me. I've run from the truth and caused untold damage every step of the way.

To Lexi's memory.

To her mother.

Even to my parents, who have no choice but to face the truth now. My dad hasn't spoken to me in over a week. When and if he will again? I have no idea. In a sense, I can't even blame him.

Living in fear is comparable to hiding beneath a security blanket, pretending all the while that if you never remove it and look beyond, the reality can't touch you. Until that blanket is ripped away, and you're forced to face everything all at once.

"I don't pay you to stare into space," comes a mocking taunt that snaps me from my thoughts.

I look up to find Rafe watching me from over the counter, his head cocked, eyes a stormy dark hue. "You're slacking."

I startle to awareness, glancing down at the same section of the floor I've been sweeping for the past five minutes. He's right—if "slacking" is synonymous with *contemplating the current state of my life."*

Compared to just a few weeks ago, the difference is night and day.

My brother is in prison.

My family is in shambles—between Kaitlin having to reconcile the truth of her marriage, and my parents coming to terms with present events and the past…

And amongst it all, I may have to testify in an upcoming trial, not to mention that I am still technically homeless.

In so many ways, I should be in a much worse state than I actually am—wearing a borrowed, oversized graphic tee and shorts, broom in hand. But for the first time, I don't feel that weight on my shoulders. That fear constantly lurking at the back of my mind has vanished.

I'm not under Branden's thumb any longer—and while my relationship with him is forever altered, at least I still have a handful of others to fall back on.

The man standing across from me, for one. And Mara. Once the news of the arrests hit the media, she was the first person to call me, even before my parents.

"Look alive, bunny," Rafe goads. Setting a stack of documents aside, he circles around to meet me. His hands find my waist, drawing me closer despite the broom held between us. "With my uncle in the slammer, I've got no choice but to be a stand-up citizen now."

"A stand-up citizen on conditional probation," I point out softly. It's the best terms, according to Liam—in exchange for him testifying against his uncle, he'll be looking at a lesser charge for any participation in criminal activity.

Which is a far brighter outlook than his uncle is facing. Branden, too, for that matter. Parallel to the investigation into his actions with Shen, the police back in PA have reopened Lexi Winacott's murder case. If everything proceeds toward its likely conclusion, then that's yet another trial I'll have to participate in.

But finally, I'll have the chance to give Lexi's mother some ounce of closure.

"So, a semi-criminal," Rafe corrects, his lip quirked. "Some people would find that a turn-on."

"A semi-criminal and a college dropout," I say with a wistful sigh. "What a pair."

He frowns. "You never mentioned anything about dropping out."

I lift one shoulder in a halfhearted shrug, but I can't meet his gaze directly. "The deadline for the Fenwick program passed. I'd rather not waste money on a useless semester."

Still frowning, he pulls away, returning behind the counter. "Funny you say that," he murmurs, lifting a stack of what looks like old mail from a drawer. From it, he withdraws a single envelope. "This came for you the other day."

Wary, I take the slim envelope, and I nearly fall over when I spy the name of my college admissions office—and judging from the fact that my old address is printed beneath my name, someone went through the hassle of collecting it for me. Whipping my gaze to Rafe, I feel my eyes widen. "You didn't."

I can't even say it out loud—turn in my essay to meet the deadline. And I have no doubt which piece of mine he chose. The one I wrote while watching him draw, feeding off his creativity.

"How did you even—"

He silences me with a kiss that takes my breath away. "You're technically still in college," he says.

Overwhelmed, I can't even challenge that assertion. "And what about you?"

"I'm an average joe with a fucking tattoo shop. The club is gone, though." He winces with genuine disappointment.

"There goes your chick magnet," I murmur. But I can't take my eyes off the acceptance letter, and the gratitude builds in my chest until it almost hurts to breathe. "I can't believe you did this—"

"I did," he says, stepping into me. "And I'll tell you how you can repay me."

My breath feathers in my chest. "How?"

"Let me tat you for real," he says against my mouth. "And then you work for me in between classes. You've got a debt to pay, remember?"

"I do," I admit, relaxing into the almost-kiss. A sudden thought makes me draw back and meet his gaze. "What kind of tat?"

He purses his lips, thinking it over, and raises one of his hands. With the tip of his finger, he traces a design over the front of my shirt. Thin, soft lines that creep down to my hips and then dip beneath the fabric entirely. My breath catches as he grazes my bare skin boldly, inching higher by the second.

"A little moth," he declares, referring to my story. What feels like his thumb grazes the flesh beneath my breast, arousing a shudder so violent my teeth chatter. "With big bunny eyes. As for the rest of your debt? You can start with writing me something new," he says, nipping my lower lip in between words. "I'm talking something way more than an essay."

I jump as he palms my breast entirely. The sensation is so distracting I can barely keep up with the thread of the conversation. Fighting for breath, I try. "Oh?"

He nods. "About you. About me… And I plan to give you more than enough fodder."

He tilts his head, deepening the kiss fully.

And I suspect that whatever story he has in mind, I'll have a wealth of inspiration to draw from.

Hey there!

Thank you so much for reading! If you enjoyed the story, please leave a review and recommend the book to any friend you think would love this twisted world. You'd have my eternal gratitude. Even a short sentence goes a long way!

Then, come join the rest of us dark romance lovers in my Facebook Group where you can get snippets, sneak peeks of upcoming books and even help vote on aspects of future novels.

Come to the dark side:

https://www.facebook.com/groups/lanasbeautifulmonsters/

WANT MORE STUFF TO READ?

Join my newsletter and get a **free book**! Plus, you get to stay updated with any new releases, random giveaways and exclusive sneak peeks!

https://www.lanaskybooks.com/newsletter

Other Novels: https://lanaskybooks.com/

Dark, Twisted Romance

Join my newsletter and get a **free book**! Plus, you get to stay updated with any new releases, random giveaways and exclusive sneak peeks!

https://www.lanaskybooks.com/newsletter

ABOUT THE AUTHOR

Lana Sky is a reclusive writer in the United States who spends most of her time daydreaming about complex male characters and parenting her Cockapoo Joey. She writes dark, twisted romance across several genres. Her titles include everything from mafia romance to vampires.

facebook.com/AuthorLanaSky

twitter.com/lanasky101

amazon.com/author/lanasky

pinterest.com/lanasky101

goodreads.com/lanasky

instagram.com/lanasky101

bookbub.com/authors/lana-sky